# DECLAN + CORALINE

*A Ruthless People Novella*

## J.J. McAvoy

This is a work of fiction. Names, characters, places, and incidents are either products of the writer's imagination or are used fictitiously and are not to be construed as real. Any resemblance to actual events, locales, organizations, or persons, living or dead, is entirely coincidental.

Declan + Coraline
Copyright © 2015 by Judy Onyegbado
ISBN-13: 978-1544897912
ISBN-10: 154489791X

NYLA Publishing
350 7th Avenue, Suite 2003, NY 10001, New York.
http://www.nyliterary.com

# TIMELINE

Declan + Coraline takes place two years before the start of Ruthless People. 23-year-old Coraline Wilson, fresh out of college, just wanted to experience life to the fullest for the first time and met 27-year-old Declan Callahan in the process. They fell hard and fast…it was their families that were the problem.

To all of you who wrote to me on

Facebook

Twitter

Tumblr,

Instagram,

Pinterest,

and

Gmail,

Asking for this book,

Thank you.

# PROLOGUE

"There's nowhere you can be that isn't where you're meant to be..."

—John Lennon

# DECLAN

"Two breakfast specials, Beatrice, and add some love in it." Liam winked at the older Irish woman who was refilling our coffees. He leaned into the booth at the Eastside Diner, while the rain that was beating against the window beside us covered all of Chicago under a dark cloud. Beatrice shook her head at him and called him a player in Irish before she took our order and left.

"You didn't sleep last night," Liam stated and I knew he was fishing.

"I'm fine—"

"You screamed for help." He frowned. "Dad stood outside your door—"

I matched his expression. "I'll tell him to stop doing that. Really, there's no need. I'm fine. The nightmares aren't as bad as they once were. You know that." Sometimes I felt like a freak in this family. Couldn't I just go to sleep for once without it being some sort of horror show?

"If you need—"

"I don't. I'm fine. Drop it, Liam."

He said nothing more and drank his coffee in silence.

Staring out the window, I found myself watching the rain. This summer had been the rainiest so far, making Chicago feel more like Seattle on some days, but worse because of the wind. I was just about to turn away when I saw a woman fighting with a broken umbrella. Because of the wind, her purse flew right off of her shoulder, and all of its contents spilled onto the ground. For some reason, I sat up as if to help her, but she gathered everything quickly and ran inside the diner for shelter. The chime of the bell above the door marked her entry to safe, dry ground.

"Dad said we're going out to the club tonight." Liam changed the subject but I couldn't look away from her as she shook the water off of her hands.

She was soaked through and through, and the green blouse she wore, along with her tight, dark jeans, clung to her body and accentuated her every curve. Her dark hair stuck to her brown face, as the rain dripped from her seductive lips. She fought with her yellow umbrella as her brown eyes glared at it in frustration.

*She's beautiful.*

"You've got to be kidding me," she exclaimed and looked at her watch.

*Was she late?*

"What are you looking at?"

"Huh?" I glimpsed back to Liam.

He stared at me before turning back to look at her. She was muttering quickly and I smirked when she laughed at herself in annoyance. *I couldn't look away from her.*

"Why are you smiling at that woman?"

"Huh?"

"That is the second 'huh' you've given me in the last minute. What did she do, steal your brain?"

"Shut up." I scowled at him as I reached for the sugar and poured it into my cup.

She shook her umbrella as if she were going to strangle it, and I found I couldn't look away from her, once again.

"Please work. *Please.*" She begged it.

*Did she know we could all see her?*

"Don't you think that's enough?"

"Huh?"

He chuckled as he nodded towards the sugar in my hands. Peeking down, I saw the mountain that had formed on the top of my drink. Dropping the sugar back on the table, I furtively snuck a peek at her; she was in her own little world.

*Seriously, what the fuck was wrong with me?*

"There's an umbrella behind you," Liam stated, still grinning as I reached behind me for it.

"Aye!" the younger freckled faced boy said as I grabbed it.

I glared at him and he swallowed slowly as he let go. "Sorry, sir, I ain't know it was you."

"No problem," I muttered as I stood up and fixed my jacket. Ignoring Liam's snickers, I walked towards her.

*Why the hell was I nervous?*

The closer I got, the more beautiful she became. She bit her full lips in determination.

"Do you need—?"

"Yes!" she almost screamed in victory as her umbrella finally opened properly.

She grinned so widely that it was contagious and I found myself smiling too. Putting the umbrella behind my back, I tried to speak to her, but without even glancing back at me, she ran out of the diner and onto the street as quickly as possible. Within moments, her yellow umbrella disappeared into the crowd and I helplessly took a step forward, as though I were going to chase after her, *but that was insane.*

"Move faster next time, brother." Liam draped his arm around my shoulder. "Too bad though. She was *really* hot."

I shrugged him off, more annoyed with myself than with him, because he was right—I'd been too slow.

"I *will* be quicker next time," I whispered, still staring at the crowd she'd disappeared into.

*I had to see her again.*

# ONE

"Their eyes met. It had begun. They had begun."

—Alexander Potter

# CORALINE

Sometimes…well most times, I felt as though everyone else was doing amazing things with their lives, while I was stuck on the sidelines. When I was twelve, I told myself, *'Just wait until I you're sixteen, then the fun will start.'* At sixteen, I said I couldn't wait for my eighteenth birthday because then my life would surely begin. Before I knew it, it was my twenty-first birthday. And now I that I was twenty-three, I'd all but given up. Yes, I was still young, but I was weird; I hated alcohol—no matter how many drinks I'd tried, they all tasted like ash to me. On top of that, large crowds made me nervous, so I was officially a buzzkill to all my friends, or I was always the one assigned to be the designated driver. I preferred to stay home unless I had to go to school, church, the bank, or to buy groceries, clothes or books. That was my life. It was made up of six places.

I'd officially graduated from Stanford three days ago and I moved back home to start working at my father's bank. Now that I was back in Chicago for the first time in four years, I'd made a resolve to try and go out again. I needed more than just six places.

Standing in front of my mirror, I curled the ends of my dark hair before I fixed my red lipstick. Then, I took a step back and smoothed out my dress.

"Can I borrow these?"

Turning, I saw my cousin, Imani, standing at my bathroom door with my brand new Brian Atwood heels in her hand.

"Imani—"

"Cora, you're like 5'9. Why do you really need heels this high? Please? Thank you!" And just like that, she was gone.

"Imani!" I yelled after her even though I knew it was no use. Whatever Imani wanted, she took.

She was only a year younger than me, but I felt like she lived a total different life than I did. While I lived in six places, Imani's world was infinite. She and I were opposites. While I was tall, dark, and all boobs, she was short, caramel skinned, and had an ass for days. Last time we'd gone out, I was literally pushed to the curb while two guys tried to ask her out.

"Ah!" I hissed, forgetting that the curling iron was still hot. Running my finger under the cold water for a moment, I turned off the iron and headed into my closet to find another pair of shoes to wear.

I ran my hand over all of my clothes and purses—all of which ranged from Prada to Alexander McQueen—and I took a seat in the middle of it all. Whenever I came into my closet, I knew that I shouldn't complain about anything. Even though both of my parents were gone, they had left me wanting for nothing for the rest of my life.

My father was the founder of Wilson International Bank, and no matter what, I would always own thirty-eight percent of it. I was better off than over ninety percent of the country—I should've been happy, I shouldn't take anything for granted.

Yet, it meant nothing to me.

"What do you think?" Imani came back and stretched out her legs so that I could see the shoes. She wore a blue dress with the sides cut out and her hair was in tight curls.

"You look good."

"I know, right? Take a picture, make sure to get everything," she said as she handed me her phone and posed in the doorway.

I took the picture and she turned and propped her hands on her waist as she puckered her lips.

"Imani, we need to go." I laughed. I took another picture before finally grabbing a simple pair of black heels.

"I'm having a few friends pick us up," she said as she checked the images on her phone.

"What? I thought it was just us, remember?"

"I know, but…" She tried not to say it.

"But I'm boring," I finished for her.

"Oh, they're here. Let's go."

"That's not an answer, Imani." I grabbed my purse, and followed her out and down the stairs. Our heels clicked against the marble as we made it to the door. I stopped and shifted the Greek vase that once belonged to my parents, as I passed by the cabinet near the doorway. My mother had gotten it while they were on their second honeymoon. It was the first thing she bought when they'd started to make money. She said Greece was filled with magic, and that I should rub the vase for good luck. I was nine, so I believed her.

Before she opened the door, she glanced at me with a serious expression. "Just don't be boring tonight, okay? Seriously, Cora, just let loose. For once in your life, just live a little."

"Okay—" I stopped when she opened the door and I saw two guys, who I didn't know, standing in front of a black Escalade. "Imani…" I began

She gave me a look before she walked up to her friends and gave them a hug.

"Derek, Otis, this is my cousin, Cora. Cora, Derek and Otis have been telling me all about this club, *The Ram*. I've been trying to get in for weeks, but it's always packed."

"Don't worry, babe, we got you," the man to her left said, as he pulled her to his side. He stood at least a good foot and a half taller than her.

"You guys ready?" Derek clapped his hands, as he looked between us.

"Don't we look ready?" Imani pouted, pulling at one of her curls. How she could be so at ease was beyond me.

"You both look *fineee*," Otis, whose voice was just a bit deeper, said, as he stretched it out. "Let's roll out."

Derek held the door for me, and with a forced smile, I slid in, all too aware that he was checking out my non-existent ass as I got inside.

"Why you ain't tell me your house was so nice, babe?" Otis said to Imani up front as we pulled out of the driveway.

"I know, right? They livin' in a gated community and shit. The security at the front all about pissed himself when he saw us." Derek laughed.

"You know, WIB, Wilson International Bank?" Imani asked.

"Yeah."

"Cora's father founded it."

"You all got it like that?" Derek looked to me.

She did a small fist pump. "Yep, if it weren't for good old Uncle Adam, we would be stuck in Southbend with y'all hoodrats."

"Well, excuse me while I change banks," Derek joked as he pulled out his phone.

"Hold up. Hold up. He coming again." Otis snickered and slowed down as we got to the front post.

Rolling down the window, I smiled at Old Man Pierre. He was in his early fifties but he had a thick black mustache above his lips. I was sure that he dyed it, but it looked good on him. He always came out of his booth to see every car.

"Ms. Wilson." He nodded to me as he looked over the car.

"Good evening, Mr. Pierre. They're friends of ours," I told

him.

He raised an eyebrow at me. "Of course. Enjoy your night, Ms. Wilson."

"You too. Be safe." I waved as we pulled out. It was only when we were far enough away that all of them broke out laughing...Imani included.

"What?"

"*Good evening, Mr. Pierre.*" They all mocked me.

"You have the strongest white girl voice I've ever heard," Imani laughed.

"You sounded like you were about to serve him tea or some shit," Derek shook his head at me.

"How should I sound?" I asked them all directly and no one had an answer. They just shrugged it off like it was nothing and I suddenly remembered why I hated going out with Imani and her friends. I always felt as though I wasn't living up to who they wanted me to be or who they thought I should be.

By the time we reached the club I was more than ready to head home. As we neared the club, I noticed the line for the Ram wrapped around the corner. Otis and Derek just led us forward.

"Boss," one of the bouncers said to Otis, as he stepped aside and let him pass.

"Boss?" Imani stopped and turned to him.

Otis shrugged his shoulders. "When I said I got you, what'd you think I meant?"

"You're lying. Y'all own the Ram?" Imani gasped as she placed her hands over her mouth.

"Southbend hoodrats are looking pretty good now, huh?" Derek did a small turn and I laughed as we went in.

The whole place was pitch black with the exception of the red and blue strobe lights. The DJ stood in front of the dance floor, with a triple X behind him as he changed up his music.

"How could you keep me out for weeks, man?!" Imani punched both of their shoulders and they grinned.

"Don't be mad. Come on, let's dance!" Otis pulled her away.

"Hold up, I got some people to see to real quick," Derek yelled over the music and into my ear.

"Of course, go ahead."

He didn't wait, and was already pushing his way through the crowd.

*Coraline, the man repellent.*

"What's wrong with me?" I muttered to myself as I once again contemplated leaving.

Since I'd already gone through the trouble of getting dressed up, I decided to stick around for just one hour, and after that, I would leave.

Pushing my way through the crowd, I made it to the bar even though I had no idea what I was going to drink.

"Can I get a Bloody Mary?" I yelled to bartender. It was the only thing I could stand to sip on.

She nodded, and bobbed her head to the beat of the music as she mixed the drink. She did it with style too. She flipped the bottle over her shoulder and even spun it before she poured it into my glass.

"Thank you!" I yelled as I reached for it. One sip and I cringed at the alcohol.

*I'm hopeless.*

I tried to force myself to keep drinking, but I just couldn't do it. The bartender must have noticed, because she came over, took the drink away from me, and switched it out for another drink.

"What is this?"

"It's alright. Just try it," she replied.

I took a small sip and laughed at myself. It was cranberry juice…and I liked it. Smiling, I lifted it up and toasted to her.

Glancing around the club, I was able to make out Derek as he stood at the far side of the club with a girl in his arms.

*I guess he found his people.* I drank slowly.

"Ladies and Gentlemen, the Callahans are in the building!" the DJ yelled, as the crowd cheered loudly.

I stood on my tiptoes, trying to see who they were, but the darkness and the mass crowd of bodies made it impossible. I remembered the Callahan name, but I wasn't sure who they were or what they did. The men around them parted the crowd, as they made their way to the VIP section of the club.

"You having fun?" Imani came up to me, drawing my

attention away from the Callahans. She grabbed my drink, took a sip, and frowned. "Seriously, Cora?"

"Don't worry about me, Imani, just go! This place is amazing!" I screamed over the music.

"Well, duh!" She headed back into the pit of bodies.

At least one of us was going to have fun.

# DECLAN

"You look lonely, sweetheart." A blonde woman in a tight blue dress that stopped mid-thigh came up to us the moment we entered the club.

Recognizing Liam, two redheads walked up to him and he placed his arms around their shoulders, as they kissed his cheeks. I rolled my eyes at him and he grinned.

Our men cleared a path through the crowd as the dancers all jumped and grinded on each other. Strobe lights lit up the dance floor, and as we made our way through, more than a few people stopped to either take pictures of us or try to get our attention while we made it towards the VIP booth. The girl on my arm posed, as she flicked her hair over her shoulder and grinned while the others looked on in envy.

Raising an eyebrow at her, I unlocked my hands from hers.

"Women like you disgust me," I said to her, and her mouth dropped in shock as I left her standing in the middle of the dance to pose for whoever else she wanted to.

"Ass!" she yelled at me, and I waved once, not caring at all.

Our men stopped anyone else from following after us.

Liam was already ordering a round of drinks as the girls around him grabbed on to his shirt, and kissed his neck. Grabbing the bottle of Cristal, I poured myself a glass.

"You're really hot." The woman in Liam's lap giggled. He nodded, clearly enjoying himself. But he knew…we both knew, that the women around us all wanted something. It was the way the world worked. They were willing to do anything for fame or money. At first it was fun. At first I was just like Liam, making out or fucking every woman who threw herself at me, but honestly I was tired of it…of them. The way they would pour their drinks on us just so they could get our attention, or pretend to trip so that we could catch them. It was all fake. I wanted something different, but did different really exist?

*I don't want to think about this.*

"Liam," I called his attention away from the woman in his lap.

He glanced up once and sighed. "Couldn't let me have five minutes?"

"Didn't know you were a five minute man." I grinned.

"Fuck you," he snapped.

"Your father would like you to handle this as soon as possible." Eric replied as he handed a slip to Liam. He looked it over quickly before his eyes met mine.

"Sorry, ladies," Liam said. "We have work to attend to. Go down and dance. We'll join you soon, I promise."

17

Liam's green eyes focused on me and he finished his glass. "You know you could try to have some fun while you're here. Instead of just brooding in the corner."

"Not interested."

"What wrong with you lately?"

I shrugged. I wasn't sure either. "Liam, aren't you bored?"

"Of Chicago? Where do you want to go? New York?"

"No, of all of this?" I pointed all around us.

"Are you insane? At twenty-five? This is the prime of my life! God knows what life will be like in…"

"In two years, after you get married? Yeah, I wonder what having an Italian wife will be like," I finished for him.

"Just because you are in a piss-poor mood doesn't mean you're going to shit on my night, you ass. Besides, you know rules, you still have to find a wife before your thirtieth birthday—"

"That's still three years away, and she doesn't have to be an Italian."

"You know what? I will handle this by myself. Before you end up as a casualty," he snapped as he stood up.

I fought the urge to laugh. "Fine, don't call on me to save your ass then!" I relaxed into the seat and grabbed a bottle.

Ignoring me, he and a few of our men went down the stairs towards the back of the club. We'd come here tonight for two reasons. First, because Liam wanted to party, and second,

18

because the owner of this club, an Otis Emerson, hadn't been paying his taxes to our family. We owned this city. It was an unspoken rule to all those downtown that a donation needed to be made in good faith before they could open any business.

Not only had this fool not done so, it was rumored that he'd spit on our family name in public. He was either an idiot or had a death wish. Either way, Liam would handle it. I planned to give him a few minutes before I went down to back him up.

"Eric, what are people saying about this place?" I asked as I looked around the club. The place was packed, and from the look of the line outside, the party was only just getting started.

"So far the reviews have been good, but you know how everyone gets excited about new places. Give it a month or two."

I nodded and he took a step back behind me. I waited a good ten minutes before I stood up and moved down the stairs to follow after Liam. I was focused on making it through the club without being touched, but I'd only made it five feet through the crowd before a drink was poured down the front of my shirt.

"Oh my God! I'm so sorry!" a woman said, already dabbing the front of my shirt with her napkin.

Honestly! Again?

Taking a deep breath, my nose flared as I smacked her hand away.

"Do not touch me!" I snapped, glaring up at her. However, the second I got a good look at her, I froze. Her long, dark, hair curled and cascaded right past her smooth, dark shoulders. The red dress she wore hugged her curves perfectly, and stopped mid-thigh, showing off her long, smooth legs.

*Diner girl!* Holy shit. I wanted to smile at her. *But was she really just like the rest of them?*

Eric went to grab her, but I held up my hand to stop him.

"I'm so sorry!" she repeated, as she looked up at me, her brown eyes wide. She wasn't scared, she was nervous and embarrassed. "I'll pay for the dry cleaning. No, I'll buy you a new one. I'm so sorry…"

"Cranberry juice?" I licked my rest of juice off my hand.

She frowned, as she dropped her head and brushed her hair behind ears. "I don't drink. I'm sorry again, Mr….?"

"You don't know who I am?" She had to be lying. "Is this part of your act?"

"My act?"

I nodded. "Pouring your drink on me to get my attention?"

She took a deep breath and gripped her purse as if she was holding herself back from hitting me. Now that would've been amusing.

"I'm sorry about your shirt. Please replace it on me." She signed a blank check and handed it to me.

*She couldn't be serious.*

However, she walked around me and disappeared into the crowd.

*What the hell just happened?*

"What happened to you?" Liam came up and I noticed that he was wearing a different shirt. He looked me up and down.

I looked back at the check.

*Miss Coraline Elizabeth Wilson.*

*Wilson International Bank.*

*317 Raven Hill Heights.*

*Run Declan, she's getting away...again!!!*

"Declan!" he yelled as I ran after her.

*She was it. She was what I'd been looking for. I couldn't let her get away.*

# CORALINE

I shivered at the feeling of the night air on my skin. I hated leaving Imani, but she'd said that she was staying over at Otis' anyway, which made me wonder what exactly she had expected me to do.

"Hey! Wait!"

Turning, I came face to face with the same green eyed, brown haired man as before. The stain on his black shirt was still slightly noticeable. Even in my heels he still had at least a good two or three inches on me. The corners of his pink lips perked up into a small smirk as he looked me over just like he did in the club.

"Are you naïve or stupid, Ms. Wilson?"

"What's your problem?" I turned to him. "I said I was sorry about your damn shirt and I promised to pay for another one. What more do you want?"

He held up the check I had given him.

"Right now, I know your full name, your account number, and your address. For all you know, you could have just earned yourself a new stalker, *Coraline.*"

I hadn't even thought about that until he'd said it.

"Well then, I'm at a disadvantage considering that you still haven't told me your name." I tried to stand up straighter.

"It's Declan," he grinned as he took a step forward. "Declan Callahan. How can you live in this city and not know that?"

"There are over two million people who live in Chicago, *Declan*. Do we all need to know who you are? Are you that vain or are you just a narcissist?"

He snickered, as his eyebrow rose. "Is there really a difference between being vain or narcissistic?"

"Is there really a difference between being naïve or stupid?" I countered.

"Touché," he said. "I suppose I owe you an apology then."

"Giving you that check was dumb idea," I muttered as I turned away from him. "So why don't we just forget this ever happened."

"Fine. But only if you go out with me for coffee."

"Now?"

He nodded. "I'll even take it as payment for the shirt."

He handed me back the blank check, and when I reached for it, he pulled it back. "Are you accepting my offer?"

"Fine. One cup of coffee."

"Good. There is a diner just down the street from here," he replied as he took my hand and led me away from the club.

The further we got from everyone, the more nervous I became. I gripped my purse tighter.

"Scared?" he asked when we stopped at the traffic lights.

"Not even a little bit," I lied. Taking a few calculated risks was all part of living, right?

"You're cute when you try to lie."

"Great. Cute was just the look I was going for," I muttered.

"You again" an older woman said as she looked at me from behind the counter when we entered the diner.

"What?"

"Seems like luck is on my side tonight, Beatrice." He winked at her as he led me to a booth. "Two coffees, and please make them as large as possible."

"What did she mean by 'you again?' "

"You don't remember?" He leaned back. "Doesn't this place look familiar to you?"

I glanced around the diner, but nothing came to mind.

"This morning you came in here soaking wet and fighting with an umbrella while you laughed at yourself."

I paused as I looked out at the dark street, and then back at the entrance.

"You also wounded my pride when I went up to you, and you ran out without even looking back."

"No way. I would have remembered you."

"Apparently you left a much more lasting impression than I did. This time I hope to rectify my past mistake, Ms. Wilson," he whispered, and I shifted under his gaze. My skin suddenly felt hot, and I was at a loss for words.

"Two large coffees," Beatrice interrupted us.

"Why large?" I tried to shift the conversation.

"You said only one coffee. I have to make it last."

"Why?"

"Why what?

"Why did you follow me outside? Why'd you ask me out for coffee?" *Why had I left a lasting impression?* But I didn't ask the last one.

"Because I thought you were beautiful from the moment I set my eyes on you, and I knew that I just had to get to know you."

*Whoa.* "Are you always this blunt?" I whispered.

"Yes." He took a sip of his coffee, and his green eyes never left mine. "Especially when it comes to things I want."

"And you seem like a man who always gets what he wants." I frowned.

"You don't seem pleased by that."

I shrugged as I grabbed my coffee as well. "I don't know much about your family, but I do remember that the Callahan boys are known for being major players."

"And you don't like being played with?"

"Who does?"

"People who play back," he countered as he sat up. "Yes. My brothers and I enjoy women. But if I only wanted to sleep with you, we would be at hotel right now, Ms. Wilson."

"You sound really confident about that. I've met men like you before, Mr. Callahan."

"People should be confident about facts, and I don't believe you've never met a man like me. However, like I said, I brought you here because I wanted to actually get to know the woman who ran away from me not once, but twice…but if you prefer a hotel—"

"There's nothing to know," I cut him off. "I'm quite boring."

"I don't believe that for a second."

"I read, shop, work, and watch movies…" I laughed as I shook my head at myself. "It's actually pretty sad. My cousin was the only reason why I came out tonight."

"I'm glad she did."

My leg brushed against his and we both froze. My heartbeat quickened.

"That was an accident!" I blurted out.

He smirked. "I'll pretend you did it on purpose. I'm not used to being a gentleman. Touch me again if it suits you."

*Why did it feel so good to touch him?* Even something as seemingly insignificant as a light brush against his leg had me wondering what his skin felt like.

"I'll keep my hands where they are." Before they got me in trouble.

"Pity." He frowned. "I really wanted to get out of this shirt."

My eyes drifted to it and I remembered how I'd gotten in this position to begin with.

"You said in there that I spilled my drink on you to get your attention. Exactly how many times has that happened?"

"Are we talking my whole life or just this month?"

"Really?"

He nodded. "I have a mass grave of all the shirts that have fallen victim to the glasses of women...and a few men too."

"How many of them have you followed outside?"

"Of the men...none, and of the women, also none. They would've had to leave for me to do that. And even then they would've had to offer to have my shirt dry-cleaned or give me a blank check...maybe both."

"All part of my master plan, Mr. Callahan," I said proudly before I sipped my coffee.

"You're sending me mixed signals, Ms. Wilson. Did you plan on getting my phone number next or were you going to discretely leave yours on the table?"

"Would you even call?"

He paused as he stared at me intensely. "Believe me, I would. But would you?"

I shrugged. "I'd think about it."

"Do much better than think. I'm not known for my patience."

"That sounds like a personal problem." I wasn't sure where this bold Coraline was coming from. It was like he was pulling this out of me, or I was feeding off of the energy he was emanating. For the first time in my life, I felt sexy…desired.

His eyes traveled down the length of my neck, to the curve of my breasts before drifting back up to my lip.

"You're tempting me," he stated.

"I'm sure it's only because you're not getting what you want." I smiled as I slid out of the booth. Before he could stand, I leaned down to him and placed my hands on his broad shoulders. "You want to fuck me, but I'm not going to allow myself to be just another woman you play with and throw to the side. Goodnight, Mr. Callahan."

I speed-walked away from him as fast I could and I stepped out of the diner and into the night. The winds blew harshly against my skin, and I only managed to make it a few more steps before his hand was on my waist. He spun me back to face him, and without wasting a moment, he kissed me hard while his other hand reached up to cup my face. I had been a kissed a few times in my life, but never like this.

I melted into him, and I moaned as my lips parted and my mouth opened for him. He greedily accepted my invitation and his tongue explored and tasted every corner of my mouth.

"Wow," I whispered as he broke the kiss and our lips parted.

"Your phone, where is it?" he questioned as his thumb pressed against my lips.

I reached into my purse without looking away from him. As

I handed it to him, he took it and stepped back without releasing my waist. Then with one hand, he dialed his number, calling himself before he hung up and gave it back to me.

"Now you can go." He released me completely and I found that I was already missing his touch.

He flagged down a taxi, and as he opened the door for me he said, "I'll be waiting on your call. Good night, Ms. Wilson."

I nodded, awe-struck and no longer able to think.

"Where to?"

"H…huh?"

"Where to, lady?"

"Raven Hill," I whispered as I turned back to stare at Declan who was still standing on the corner, watching me as I watched him. My hands went to my lips.

"Wow."

*What just happened?*

# TWO

"You may not believe in magic, but something very strange is happening at this very moment."

—Leonora Carrington.

# CORALINE

*"Did you get home okay?"* I reread the text message he'd sent over twenty minutes ago.

I couldn't bring myself to reply. My head was still spinning. It was three a.m. and I couldn't stop thinking about how hard his body felt as it was pressed against mine and how nice the kiss had been. No. *Nice* wasn't the word—sinful, sexy, and delicious—that's what came to mind.

*Get yourself together, Coraline!*

I wasn't that person…the bold, sexy Coraline he'd met tonight wasn't me, and I had no idea where she'd come from or how she came into being.

*I should text him back, right?*

*"I got home fine. Thanks. Hope you did as well. You were nice tonight."*

Send.

Wait! No! *"You were nice tonight?"* What the hell did that mean? I threw the phone aside and buried my face in the pillow.

*BUZZ*

The second I heard it, I jumped towards the phone.

*"Nice wasn't what I was going for, but at least I finally made an impression."*

33

*"What where you going for?"*

*"Passionate?"*

I smiled. *"Mission accomplished."*

*"I bet you say that to all the guys. So, you were the Valedictorian at Stanford?"*

"How did you know that?" I whispered to myself. Before I could text him back, he sent an explanation in two consecutive messages. It was as though he knew I would be taken aback by his question.

*"It was the first thing I that came up when I Googled you."*

Followed by…

*"I Googled you because I couldn't get you out of my mind."*

Reaching for my laptop on the other side of the bed, I Googled him too, and frowned at the very thing I saw.

*"The first thing that came up on you was that a Victoria's Secret model confessed to being in love with you."*

This was why I shouldn't have texted him in the first place. I was way out of my league here. When I tried to click on the article, a 404 error message came up. Going back to the home page, the article was gone and I wondered if I had imagined the whole thing.

"What the hell?" I yawned to myself.

BUZZ

*"We all have a past, Coraline. Get to know me before first before you decide who I am."*

*"I will. Good night…again."* I held the phone to my chest as I drifted off to sleep…thinking of him.

\*\*\*

It was Sunday morning and Aunty Trisha, who was still in her robe with curlers in her hair, and Uncle Adam, who was nursing a hangover with some soup, were already self-medicating.

"What is this?" I held up the bill in my hand.

"Coraline, go yell somewhere else this morning," my aunt mumbled, as she handed a cup of coffee to my uncle before she sat down.

"You spent almost forty grand in the last three weeks! On what? I just gave you money!"

"Coraline!" my uncle snapped at me. "Not now."

Now was never the right time for them.

I put the bills back onto the table.

"I'm going to mass. We'll talk about this later," I said on my way out, and, like always, they spoke just loud enough for me to hear.

"What's wrong with that girl?"

"Honey—" my aunt began.

"Money. Money. Money. She didn't say anything when she flew herself to California! Don't you forget that Wilson is my last

35

name too! If her father wasn't so damn greedy, I would've had my share!"

Ignoring him, I walked into the garage, and flicked on the lights. Grabbing the keys to my grey Infiniti, I pulled out as quickly as possible. I hadn't even been home for a week and I was already tired of dealing with them. It was so much easier when I was far away. I could pretend to not get their messages or calls for a little while and it would force them to live off of what they already had.

*Why did I move back?* I'd asked myself this question at least hundred times in the last five days. But I knew that the answer was that they were the only family I had left. No grandparents, no parents, no siblings, just them. I could take their abuse, but I couldn't take the loneliness.

That was why I came back to Chicago. Besides, when you grew up here, it was kind of hard to leave. The city had its way of growing on you…the city of the wind. Sometimes if you stood still long enough, it felt as though those winds could pick you up and take you anywhere.

I was ten minutes early, but the parking lot for St. Peter's Cathedral was already nearly full. A row of black luxury cars was parked in front; one Rolls-Royce, one Bentley, an Audi and an Aston Martin. It said something when the most discrete car in the lot was an Audi. Shaking my head, I grabbed my things, and turned my phone off as I walked inside.

I stopped at the church's wall of donors, which stood right outside the second double doors that led inside. Smiling to myself, I ran my hand over the gold plate that had my parents' names on it.

"Hi Mom and Dad," I whispered before I headed inside.

I wasn't religious, but I came because I knew they would've have wanted me to. I entered the packed church and took a seat in the back between an old woman and little boy.

"Hello," I said to the cutie as I grinned. He smiled and hid his face in his father's chest. Smiling at him, I, along with everyone else, stood as the priest came forward. I usually zoned out after this part, as I went through the motions of it all, however, my mouth dropped open as none other than Declan Callahan, dress in a fitted navy suit and silver tie, headed up towards the podium do the first reading.

"Sit," the little boy next to me said as he pulled on my dress.

Realizing that I was the only one still standing, I sat down quickly and hoped that no one else had noticed. Unfortunately, the one person I wish hadn't, did. Declan looked me straight in the eye and cocked an eyebrow. All I could do was grab the book in front of me and pretend to read.

"Proverbs 21:19-26. It is better to live in a desert land than with a *quarrelsome* and *fretful* woman." As he read, he stretched out words certain words, and if I didn't know better, I would've thought that he'd chosen this passage just to poke fun at me. He couldn't even wipe the grin from his face.

*I loved the sound of his voice.*

The moment the thought hit me, I tried to block him out. Luckily, he had finished his reading and was already walking away from the altar, and back down to the first row.

Of all the churches in the city, why did he have to come to this one? And why didn't I just sit down?

I tried not to think about him or anything else for that matter. That only lasted for a good thirty minutes or so. Before we all stood for the Eucharist, he came into view again. He stood off to the side with a golden tray in his hand. To my dismay, the lines divided and I soon found myself heading towards him like the Titanic towards an iceberg. There were too many people behind me to change lines, and when his green eyes focused on mine, I felt as though he was pulling me to him…it was the same feeling I'd had when I'd sat across from him at the diner.

"The body of Christ," he said with a smile, as he held the host up.

"Amen," I whispered as I stretched out my hands.

But he didn't place it inside and I glared at him, waiting. His eyes shot to the older woman in other line, who opened her mouth for the priest.

He must be joking.

But he clearly wasn't. Dropping my hands, I opened my mouth for him.

He placed the Sacramental bread on my tongue, but not before his finger grazed my lips causing me to shiver. He spared me one glance, but he didn't say anything. Finally, he picked up another one and looked to whoever was behind me.

Walking away, I touched my lips slowly as I looked back to him.

*Not again.* There was no way I could be attracted to him this much. This wasn't normal, right? It'd been a long time, but a man's touch shouldn't have confused me this much. Taking a seat, I crossed my arms and legs as I waited for the mass to come to end.

*I should just walk away. He's just playing around.*

"Bye-bye," the little boy said as he waved to me.

"Sorry he was such a bother," his mother said as she picked him up.

"No, it was fine." In fact I hadn't really noticed him. Nodding to me, her son kept waving as they headed to out. "Bye-bye!"

"Friends of yours?"

Startled, I turned to find that Declan was no more than an inch away from me.

"I waited all day yesterday for you to call," he said, and I watched as his eyes drifted from my eyes to my lips to my neck and then to my chest. "I've never waited for a woman to call, or have a woman reject mine."

"I was busy," I lied.

He frowned and looked me over as though he could see through my lie.

"Do you have a boyfriend, Coraline?" he asked me as we walked towards the exit.

"What?"

"Do. You. Have. A. Boyfriend?" he repeated.

We were outside and Father Thomas was already making the rounds and greeting everyone.

"Why?"

"Just wondering if that was the reason you didn't call. And if it is, how hard am I going to have work?" he asked as he stuck his hands into his pocket.

He was by far the most direct man I had ever met in my life.

"What are you trying to work for, Mr. Callahan?"

He smirked. "Our date, of course."

"And if I have a boyfriend?" I whispered still unsure if this was a dream or reality. Men like him weren't real, or at least for me, they weren't.

"I would steal you away in front of him," he said, as he closed the gap between us.

He blocked the sun as he stood before me; all I could see was him. But I didn't want to give into him.

"And what if I have a fiancé?"

"I would steal you away right under his nose. After all, it

would be his fault for not giving you a ring."

I hid my hands behind my back.

"And if I have a husband?"

"Then you've made a terrible mistake. And once we've rectified the situation, I'd have you," he whispered as he brushed my hair behind my ear. "Are we done with this game now, Ms. Wilson?"

"I have to give it to you, Mr. Callahan, you are smooth." I smiled brightly as I took a step back.

"But you still aren't convicted about me," he stated and under his breath. And I could have sworn he added, "You have some instincts." But I wasn't sure, maybe it was my own subconscious talking to me.

I looked away. "Like I said, I've met men like you before."

"And like *I* said—no you haven't."

I glanced back at him to find that his eyes were still on me. "Thank you for being interested me in, Declan. Seriously, it's the best I've felt about myself in a while. But I—I'm not the dating type."

"Okay. Walk away. But don't look back or else I won't give up on you," he said.

"Okay." I nodded as I walked around him.

*Don't look back.*

*Don't look back.*

*Coraline, don't look back!* I begged myself as I grabbed on to the door handle of my car.

"Coraline!"

I turned back and he grinned only a few feet away from me.

"That's cheating!"

"According to who? The rule was *don't look back*, I never said I wouldn't call out to you. Do people really give up so easily in your world?"

Yes. And I couldn't deny the part of me that was happy that he'd called out to me.

"Are people always this stubborn in your world?"

"Sweetheart, I'm Irish. They don't come any more stubborn than that." He pushed my car door closed, preventing me from getting in. "And since you looked back, let's go somewhere."

"I'm busy."

"That was your excuse for not calling yesterday. Besides it's Sunday, you shouldn't be working. You just came back to Chicago, I should show you everything you've missed out on."

"Chicago hasn't changed that much."

"That's where you are wrong. Chicago changes every night."

I bit my lip hard, unsure of what I should do…or at least my mind was unsure, my body however, turned towards him.

"It's not a date," I clarified.

He nodded. "Sure. It's not a date."

"Then I'll drive myself—"

"Waste of gas. Come on." He took me by the hand and

dragged me towards his dark gray Aston Martin. I held on to his hand just as tightly as he held on to mine. When he opened the door for me, I slid into the passenger seat and dropped my bag next to my feet. He spoke to someone next to the Audi for a brief moment before he stepped inside.

"Is everything okay?" I glanced back at the young man with messy dark brown hair and green eyes who stood staring at the car.

"Don't worry. My brother, Liam, just wanted to go out," he replied as he reversed out of the parking lot.

"You shouldn't ditch him—"

"He wants to go a fashion show and pick up models. Why would I do that when you're sitting right next to me?"

I didn't answer as I looked out the window. What was I doing in his car?

"Who was he?" he asked.

"What?"

He didn't look at me, but focused on the road ahead.

"The guy who hurt you? Who was he?"

"No one."

There was silence for a moment before he spoke. "Just so you know, you are horrible at lying."

*I know.*

He pulled to a stop at Millennium Park.

"If there's anything in Chicago that hasn't changed, it's

Millennium Park." It was the biggest tourist attraction in Chicago.

"Trust me," he stated as he stepped out and around to my side, but I opened the door for myself much to his disappointment. He took of his tie and suit jacket, and threw them into the car. After he'd rolled up his sleeves, he held my hand like it was the most natural thing in the world; like he had done it a thousand times before and would do it a thousand times again. He led us into the park, and surprisingly, it wasn't as crowded as I thought it would be.

He kept going until we were standing at Cloud Gate, or *the Bean* as everyone called the steel bean-shaped sculpture in the park. When we got there, a small crowd had gathered around a band.

"Three, two, one!" they yelled as they started to clap along with the crowd. The best way to describe it would have be '80s or '90s funk, and soon, everyone started dancing.

"Are we in flash mob?!" I gasped, looking to him.

He bobbed his head, dancing as well, then he pulled us closer to the front.

"I don't know what I'm doing!" I laughed.

"Then do anything!" he yelled back.

Not dancing would have only made me stick out more. Giving in, I jumped around him. He didn't let go of me, as he spun me around.

"I can't hear you!" the lead singer yelled.

I screamed as loud as I could until I was afraid my voice would crack. Then, with a broad smile, I threw my hands up and swayed to the beat of the music.

"You look even more beautiful when you smile," he said to me, and I froze in the midst of the crowd. "No. Keep dancing, keep smiling or screaming, whichever suits you best. Be this happy all the time, Coraline."

I didn't believe in magic, or in happily ever after. Life to me didn't work that way, and yet as I watched him dance around me, I couldn't help but believe in it just a little. It was like time had slowed down for me so that I could just enjoy this one moment. I had spent my entire life wishing for something like this, wishing to be whisked away, and to simply live life as I felt it should be lived. So why then did I feel the compulsion to run away from what I always wanted? Why was I fighting my own happiness?

"Declan?"

"Yeah—?"

I kissed him. Hoping to kiss him just like he'd kissed me. He stilled for a moment before he wrapped his arms around me and deepened the kiss while the music continued blaring in the background. I leaned into it enjoying the moment…enjoying him. I was still unsure if he was merely a figment of my imagination. If he was it didn't matter. I would believe in magic…if only for today.

# DECLAN

In one minute—

Roughly 1,800 stars explode.

Lightning strikes the earth 360 times.

Two hundred and fifty people are born.

One hundred and seventy people die.

And then I realized, without knowing anything else besides the fact that she was beautiful, that she had a breathtaking smile, and that her kisses felt like fresh rain in the desert, I knew that Coraline Wilson would be in my life for a long time.

It was insane. But I just knew that that was how it had to be.

"Declan?" she whispered when she broke away from me. I hadn't realized that I was staring at her, but I could see my reflection in her eyes.

"Sorry. I was lost in thought."

"About what?"

Luckily, I didn't have to answer since the police suddenly rushed into the park and began grabbing people as they tried to run away.

"Until next time, guys!" The band laughed as they rushed to grab their things and make a run for it.

I held on to her, making sure she didn't get pushed around as the crowd broke up as well.

"Why are they breaking them up?" She frowned. "I really liked them."

"Musicians can't play here, it's against the law. Don't worry though, they'll be back," I reassured her.

She turned to see that they were all still running and she screamed, "Free the music! Keep going!"

She laughed as she brushed her hair behind her ear. Then her beautiful eyes drifted back to me. Neither of us spoke. We simply stood there holding on to each other as everyone else went back to their own reality. I was worried that the spell, or whatever it was that was happening between us, would stop. Every one of my senses were aware of her. She smelled like lavender, looked more beautiful than the beginning of spring at the end of harsh a winter...she made me think of a dozen other cheesy things all within those few moments.

I spun her around to face me, and I leaned forward and kissed her once again and never wanted to stop.

## CORALINE

We made it to his car, and the second we got in, I jumped onto his lap. His seat reclined until we were laying down, and his hands found their way under my skirt. My skin was on fire and all I could think was, 'screw it.' If he dumped me after he'd gotten what he wanted, then I'd rather it happen sooner instead of later, because the truth of the matter was that I was already beginning to fall for him.

If it was meant to be just sex, I could handle that now.

"Ah, Declan," I moaned his name.

He squeezed my ass and bit, licked, and kissed my neck, while my hands fought with the buttons of his shirt...an action that was more patient than what he did with mine. Grabbing the front of my button-down shirt, he ripped it open and sent the buttons flying everywhere.

I stared down at him and gasped as he pulled my bra down and took my nipple into his mouth.

"Oh," I gasped as I shifted on top of him.

Though his pants were still on, I could feel his hard cock through my sheer underwear as I grinded myself against him.

*I wanted to feel him.*

My hands pulled at his belt and I undid his pants and freed his erection. He throbbed in my hand and twitched with excitement when my thumb rubbed his tip.

"Fuck, Cora," he hissed as he licked his lips.

I bit his bottom lips softly then kissed him once more. My hands slowly ran along the length of him, and he bucked his hips upward, thrusting into my hand. His eyes never left mine as his hand drifted between my thighs, slid into my underwear, and rubbed against me just as slowly.

My mouth dropped open, as my breathing grew ragged and uneven.

"Declan." I squeezed his member as two of his fingers entered me. He fucked me with his fingers as I worked him in my hands. I enjoyed his every moan and the fact that he seemed to grow even harder in my hands.

We kissed each other again, but it wasn't gentle or wet. It was, passionate, sinful, and full of lust. Our tongues collided and we moaned into each other's mouth.

"C...Cora." He gasped when we broke away.

"I want you." I licked my lips.

"I'm in your hands," he replied as he pulled his fingers out of me, and I watched as he licked my essence off his fingers. Before I could give it any thought, I leaned in lick as well.

"You are beyond sexy." He groaned.

But I wasn't. This wasn't me. He had done this. He'd made

me this way, and I couldn't control myself. I didn't want to control myself.

Shifting upwards, my breasts pushed up against his face and he tenderly kissed each of them. I positioned myself above him and smiled as I allowed the head of his cock to part my wet folds.

"Stop teasing me," he demanded.

"I like teasing you." I kissed his nose as I rubbed myself on top of him.

"Coraline."

"Yes?" I asked as I slowly lowered myself onto him.

"Goddamn it," he hissed as he grabbed my waist and thrust upwards and into me.

"Fuck." I gasped as my mouth fell open and a wave of pleasure rushed through me. I couldn't stop myself. My hands went to his shoulders and I began to bounce and rock against him. He held onto my waist and thrust into me, matching each one of my movements.

There was such little space in the car in that I had to rest my head against his. His green eyes never drifted away from mine, and I enjoyed myself as I rode him.

I closed my eyes. I couldn't...

"N...No," he said breathing heavily. "Don't look away from me, Coraline, please."

It was like my body did whatever he wanted...my eyes opened and I watched him as the pleasure continued to build up.

Climax wasn't far off, and as we lost ourselves in each other, I couldn't help but think that he was the sexy one.

"So...t...tight," he groaned, as his grip on me tightened.

My hands went to his bare chest as I braced myself, and I relished in the feel of his hard muscles under my fingers.

"Faster," I said, more to myself than to him as I rose and fell on top of him.

The sound of skin against skin and our moaning blended into one, as the smell of sex filled the car with every thrust.

*So good!* It was the only thing running through my mind over and over again.

"Harder." I bit my lip as he pushed me up against the steering wheel. The horn blared, but neither of us noticed as we fucked each other.

"Declan!" I cried out. My hands reached upwards as I braced myself against the roof of his car, while my eyes rolled back into my head as I came.

He placed his head on my stomach, and a series of curses and grunts fell from his lips as he thrust deeper.

"Fuck, Cora. Ah!" he managed to say as he found his release as well.

Neither of us said anything as we collapsed onto each other. He refused to let me go, and truthfully, I didn't want him to.

All that talk about not wanting to be another one of the women he just screwed and I'd only manage to last three days before I fucked him in his car.

*So classy, Coraline, at the end of the day, it seems that you really aren't any different after all.*

# DECLAN

We drove back to the church in silence and I tried to not be distracted by the fact that I had ruined her shirt. She had to fold her hands over her chest to keep it closed. But I didn't want her to. I needed to see her skin again. I wanted to run my tongue over it. I needed more. I had never wanted more.

I should have wanted her to leave and to never have to talk about this again, but that was the last thing I wanted. I hated car sex…I preferred to dominate my women and I couldn't have her the way I wanted…the way I needed.

*She was amazing though. Did she enjoy it too? What was I thinking, I was sure she did. But what if she didn't?* My eyes drifted to her again and my heart started to beat faster. I forced myself to look away.

*What the hell was wrong with me?*

"Thanks." It was all she said when we reached the church. The parking lot was now completely empty, though she still glanced around, as she held her shirt closed, to make sure no one was around. Reaching behind me I grabbed my coat and handed it to her.

"No, it's okay—"

"Take it, Coraline, just in case."

She nodded it and I shivered when her hand brushed against mine as she took it from me. She slipped it on and stepped out of the car.

*We couldn't just end like this.*

I got out of the car and called after her. "Coraline!"

She stopped without turning around.

"Coraline!" I called her name again and smiled when she refused to turn back. After all, that was how we'd gotten this far to begin with.

"Declan." She finally faced me with small, fake smile. "It's over. We both got what we wanted. The clock struck midnight and the magic is gone. Now we can go our separate ways."

I frowned as I stepped towards her and shook my head.

"Coraline, the story doesn't end when the clock strikes midnight. That's when it starts and we have to make our own magic."

She smirked, shook her head at me, and opened her door.

"Goodbye, Mr. Callahan."

She started her car and drove away without another word.

Sitting back in mine, I took a deep breath. Dialing, I waited for him to answer.

"Mother isn't happy that you missed Sunday brunch," Liam stated.

"I kissed her Liam. On Friday and again today, before we had sex."

There was a moment of silence before he spoke. "You kissed her…on the lips?"

I nodded even though he couldn't see. "Yeah."

"I thought that was your line in the sand. You never kiss them on the lips, Declan. You fuck them and leave…you've been like that since we were teenagers."

"That's the problem…with her there is no line in the sand, Liam. I want to see her again."

"Why are you so hung up on her? You don't know anything about her."

"I don't, but she's different." That was the only thing I could think of. "She is beautiful, smart, and different. Do I really need any other reason to be attracted to her?"

"Attracted? No. Obsessed? Yes. Especially when you know that it can never become anything more than a fling. She's not one of us, Declan, so just get it out of your system before Father catches on that this is more than just some screw for you."

How could I get her out of my system when every time I was near her I just wanted to touch her more?

"Declan."

"Yeah."

"Stay away from the good girls. We either break them, or they break us. And just in case you were wondering, I took care of the club owner and got the tax. Father is looking into them and he might need us. Don't forget who you are what you do," he said before he hung up. I hated it when he got serious.

Logic told me he was right and that I *should* stay away from Ms. Coraline Elizabeth Wilson. She had a clean record and had never even gotten a speeding ticket. She went to church. She didn't drink, and at first, I'd thought she was an alcoholic...I would have preferred it actually. But no matter how hard I tried, I couldn't find anything that indicated she was. All the comments on her graduation speech were from people congratulating her, and saying that a better person couldn't have earned it. In our family good people were chess pieces...disposable. It was the way it needed to be.

*Why am I even thinking of the family? We hadn't even gone out on a proper date yet.*

*Why was I thinking of a proper date?*

"Declan, get yourself together," I told myself for the umpteenth time since I'd met her.

# THREE

"Take time to deliberate, but when the time for action comes, stop thinking and go in."

—Napoléon Bonaparte

# CORALINE

I'd kept my phone turned off for the last two days. I didn't want to stare at it, wondering whether or not he would call, when I already knew the answer to that. So my plan was to do what I came to Chicago to do in the first place—work. I was now in the corner office of WIB, looking out at the Chicago skyline. At twenty-three I was officially able to take part in every meeting, have own office, and my own staff. Who needed anything else?

*Who needed Declan Callahan?*

"Come in," I said loudly to the office door.

"Ms. Wilson?" Tyrone Stevens, the second youngest board member, entered my office. He was dressed in a blue-striped suit and was at least a decade older than me. He stood just about an inch or two shorter than me, and his skin was a shade darker than mine.

His dark brown eyes looked me over. "I heard you'd set up an office and I wanted to say hello earlier, but work got in the way." He held out his hand and I shook it as I smiled.

"Thank you, Mr. Stevens. It's really good to be here."

"I was just a high school intern when your father started this business. I'm sure he's proud of you. You're a remarkable young woman."

"Don't flatter me too much. At least not until I've earned it."

He nodded. "Of course. If you need anything, please don't hesitate to ask me."

"I'll keep that in mind, but I really hope I don't need to come running to you just yet," I replied feeling slightly awkward under his gaze.

I waited for him to say something more, but he didn't.

"Did you need anything else?" I prompted.

"No. Sorry. I'll let you get back to work. Again, welcome to your bank."

I laughed. "Thank you."

He stepped back to door, and before it could close completely, my secretary peeked her head inside. Her glasses slid down her nose and she pushed it back up as she waited for me to acknowledge her.

"Yes?"

"Your uncle his here. I told him you weren't seeing anyone, but he says he won't leave until—"

"It's okay, Constanza, let him in."

But before she could, Uncle Adam burst into my office. "What did I tell you? If you had a brain—"

"Uncle!" I cut him off as I rushed to the door. "I'm so sorry, Constanza. If anyone else asks for me, please tell them I'm a meeting."

She nodded and I closed the doors before I turned to him.

"Do not insult my staff!" I snapped.

He snorted as he walked up to the windows. "Your staff? Look at you, you sound just like your father. Next will come your work, your company, and your money. Here I am repeating history to a child."

I took a deep breath. "What do you want?"

"Did you know we started this company together? We were just bookies as first, hustlers on the streets. Your father was the brains, I had the street smarts, the charm. Getting people to trust me was just so easy. *Too easy.* Then he started investing...without me. He doubled their money not only on paper, but in their actual hands. Next he was buying offices...without me. This business, it grew out of thin air. I couldn't believe it. I thought we'd finally made it and then I tried to walk into the office one day and a girl, the same age as you said I couldn't go up...not without an appointment. You should have seen my face." He turned and glared around the office and I could see the tension in his jaw as he gnashed his teeth together. "That's when I realized that brains outdid charm. He screwed me right out of everything and there was nothing I could do about it—"

"Uncle." I sighed. "I know this story. You've told me it almost every day since he died."

"Good riddance too! He was a fucking bastard!"

I took a quick breath like he'd stabbed me. No matter how many times he said it, it still hurt. I wanted to scream that he was my father for better or worse, but I knew that it would only make my uncle rant more.

"Do you need more money, Uncle?" I just wanted him to go.

He snickered bitterly. "You little...No. I didn't come for money! I came for my cut, it's past time I got what was owed to me. This place wouldn't have been built if it weren't for the connections and the deals I made!"

"You know I can't do that."

"Why not? Aren't you a major shareholder?"

"It doesn't work like that—"

"Then make it, Coraline! Make up for your father's sins! We are family. I've taken care of you since you were a child. You have no one else but me. Your actual blood is my blood, how can you turn away from away that?"

Nodding, I tried not to cry. I hated when he manipulated me like this. "I'll work on something for you here and we will work on the board together, but you have to get your act together, Uncle. You can't just blow through money."

He beamed as he rushed over to me and gave me a small hug. "That's my girl."

"Go home, Uncle. I will have you here by the end of the week," I whispered. And against my better judgment, I hugged him back.

"Yeah, okay. Don't let me down." He let go of me and left my office.

I felt like a child again. The only time I ever got love or affection from him or anyone else in my family was when they were taking something from me.

But we were family.

With a sigh, I moved back to my chair, and as I fell against it, I leaned back and closed my eyes.

*You're okay, Coraline. You're fine. You don't need their affection. You're fine.*

"Ms. Wilson?"

*Couldn't I get a second to think?! Jeez!*

"Yes, Constanza." I opened my eyes and kept looking up at the ceiling.

"You know the new investor?"

I sat up. "Kelly Laoghaire?"

She nodded at the door. As of this morning we'd received close to eighty million dollars from the Laoghaire trust.

"Send them in!" I said quickly as I fixed my hair, and smoothed out my dress.

I was already moving towards the door, ready to greet them, when Declan Callahan stepped into my office, wearing a fitted suit, and a smile that spread across his face.

"It's a pleasure to meet you, Ms. Wilson," he said as he held out his hand to me.

I stood there, too dumbfounded to move…and a little too happy to see him as well.

# DECLAN

By the time she got over her shock, I was already siting in one of the chairs in front of her desk. To say that I was impressed would've been an understatement. Her office was simple, classic, and elegant. The walls behind her desk displayed her degrees and awards, and I could only imagine how hard she must have worked to be able to get a corner office on the top floor.

"Kelly Laoghaire?" she whispered as she walked to the side of her desk. Her dress was far too tempting; the golden zipper that ran from the back of her neck all the way down to her ass made my hand twitch.

"Yes. Kelly Laoghaire. It was my mother's name before she became Kelly Callahan."

"The money?" She slowly processed.

"The money they left to me before they passed away. Once again, *I'm in your hands*, Ms. Wilson."

Her mouth parted and I wished it hadn't because all I could think of was wanting to hear her moan.

She shook her head at me as she took a seat in her leather chair like a queen on her throne.

"Why are you doing this?"

"I've been looking for place to invest in. Why not you?"

"Why do I have a feeling that this is about more than just my bank?"

She was holding herself back, I could see it the way she crossed her legs, and in the way her eyes drifted from my lips to my neck and back to my eyes again before they completed the circuit once more.

I smirked. "Because you're smart. In all honesty though, I came here because I couldn't reach you on your phone."

"Maybe I didn't want to be reached."

"Maybe you were worried I wouldn't try to reach. Maybe you're afraid you will like spending time with me, or maybe even love it. "

She paused and I knew that I was right.

*I should have come earlier. Why was I always so slow when it came to her?*

"That's a whole lot of maybes, Mr. Callahan."

"Fine. Allow me to clarify then. I came to clear up any confusion between us."

"So this is what you meant by making your own magic?"

I shrugged. "I do what I can with what I've got."

"Declan, I am not Cinderella."

"Good, because I'm not Prince Charming. I prefer black." I was referring to my clothes, but the smile that crept onto her face proved that she had taken a dual meaning.

"You aren't playing by the rules."

"Of course not. I'm a Callahan, we make our own rules, so you might as well get used to it now."

"Declan, we had sex, and it was great. So why not end this on a high note and just walk away?"

"Because I have no desire to, and I always do what I desire. You should too. I honestly have no idea why you're fighting this so hard."

She didn't answer and I hoped it was because she didn't have an answer.

"You don't take rejection well, do you?"

"No. But you haven't rejected me. Instead you've put me at arm's length. You pulled me in, fucked me, and pushed me out again. And since I had to hand over eighty million dollars just to see your face again, you could at least take me out to lunch…"

"Declan—"

"Don't think of it as a date, think of it as a client luncheon. I thought you were all prepared to make nice with *Kelly Laoghaire?* You almost jumped me when I walked in before you realized who I really was."

"Fine. Where would you like to go? And since this is a client luncheon, I'll pay."

"Surprise me, Ms. Wilson."

She nodded and reached under her desk for her bag before rising. Following her out. My eyes were glued to her ass, and judging by the way she added a little extra sway to her step told me that she knew it too. She closed her door, spoke to her secretary, and then silently walked to the elevator with me.

She was so close.

"Ms. Wilson?"

We both turned to the black man who was handing an armful of files over to her secretary.

"Mr. Stevens, meet Declan Callahan, owner of the Laoghaire trust," she stated.

His eyes widened and he reached out to shake my hand. "It's a pleasure to meet you."

"Likewise." *Not really.* I shook his hand.

"We were just about to head to lunch."

I glanced at her. *Do not invite him.*

"Really? My schedule—"

"Mr. Stevens, thank you, but I'm sure I can handle it," she said with her head held high.

The elevator doors opened behind us and we stepped in.

"We'll talk when you get back," he said.

"Of course. Thank you again—"

I pressed the doors close.

"Declan."

"He has a thing for you." And I didn't like it at all.

"No, he doesn't." She shook her head and laughed as if it were impossible.

She was clueless as to the effect she had on men. Before he realized who I was, he'd looked at me with a mixture of annoyance and jealousy. His eyes were filled with lust the second they'd fallen on her.

For a split second I thought of them together, and as if to claim her I put my hand on her ass.

"Declan."

"If you don't like it, then tell me to let go."

She didn't say anything, but glanced up at the cameras instead.

"Those things don't have audio," I replied before I squeezed a handful of her ass, enjoying how firm it felt in my hand.

"If they weren't there at all I would push you up against the wall, and kiss from your lips down to your—"

"D…Declan," she said softly.

"Just like that. You would call out my name just like that. There are ninety-eight floors in the building? I wonder if I could make you come before we reached the bottom. Would my hands be enough? Or better yet, my tongue?"

"Stop it," she said, and I let go of her ass as I fixed my tie.

"Why? Is it because you were wondering the same thing?"

She didn't answer. Instead she fixed her skirt. It funny how we both felt the need to fix our clothes even though we hadn't done anything. Maybe it was because we were already fucking each other in our minds.

71

And in my mind, the elevator never reached the bottom.

## CORALINE

"Absolon, nice choice," he replied as he unfolded his napkin, and one of the waiters, upon noticing, came over and placed a one thousand dollar bottle wine on the ice in front of us before greeting him.

Damn it. I wanted this to be my moment to show him...to show him that I was a lot classier than a car screw in the park. But he seemed well at home, like he had been to one of the most expensive restaurants in the city so many times it didn't faze him.

"Mr. Callahan," I tried to sound professional even though I kept thinking about how nice it would feel to be on top of him again. "These are just some of my thoughts on how I intend to triple the money you've in invested with us. If you have any concerns, please let me know."

I handed him the file. He took it and put it to the side. "Thanks, but I'm sure you'll take care of it."

"Are you really this naïve or just stupid?" I countered, using his own words against him.

He smirked. "Neither. Like I said, I trust that you will take good care of me."

73

I wanted to say don't trust me but that it wouldn't have been wise. He and I both reached out for the water and our hands brushed together. I quickly drew mine away, worried that he'd notice how excited I'd gotten by that simple touch.

"Tell me about the Laoghaire trust." I picked up my menu.

"I'd rather not," he said, and I glanced back up at him. "I rather tell you about me. My name is Declan Callahan, and I enjoy fine wine, finer women, and sex."

*I wanted him so bad.*

"If you want to woo a girl, don't you usually say something romantic?"

"It seemed pretty romantic to me since I have everything I enjoy right here."

Damn, he was good.

"We aren't having sex."

"Baby, we've been having sex from the moment I walked into your office," he whispered.

*Please take me.*

I crossed my legs under the table, trying to get a grip on myself. He noticed. How could one man make me want to forget everything and just jump him over and over again? I kept telling myself that I wasn't this person, but I wasn't sure anymore.

"Are you ready or would you like a moment?" the waiter asked as he came over to us.

"No!" I sat up as I answered. But the problem was that I had no idea what I wanted.

"May I?" Declan asked and I nodded. He glanced up at the waiter. "She'll have the Teriyaki Salmon Rice with sliced mushrooms, not grounded, on the side. The glaze should go over the fish not the rice, and her drink…" He paused and looked to me. "Pair it with the best virgin you can think of. I'll have sirloin, done the way I like it, Kevin."

"Of course, Mr. Callahan." He nodded.

"Impressed?" Declan asked as he lifted his glass of water to his lips.

"So you can order food. If you gave me five more minutes I'm sure I would have ordered the same thing." I shrugged nonchalantly.

He snickered. "I'm sure of it. So, tell me more about you, *Coraline*.

"There is nothing more to tell—"

"So you're saying that I know everything about you right now?"

"Fine. My name is Coraline Elizabeth Wilson. I'm an only child, I live with my uncle and aunt at Raven Hill Heights…"

"Get more personal," he whispered as he leaned in. "Who are you, Coraline Elizabeth Wilson? I've been trying to figure it out on my own, but I just can't seem to answer that question."

"Personal?"

"Why are you afraid to let yourself have fun with me?"

"Because I don't know how to have fun, Declan. I'm not like you. I need a man I can depend on, not a man who wants to turn me on in elevators."

"Why can't you have both?"

Why couldn't I? Because... "Both doesn't exist."

"In my world, it does," he stated.

I shook my head. "We live in the same world, Declan—"

"That's where you are wrong. While it's true that we share the same planet, trust me when I say that we all live in different worlds. The way I was raised was when a man takes a woman, he takes care of her, he protects her, he fights for her, and he sure as hell ensures that she's turned on no matter where she is. The Irish would disown me if I did otherwise."

"And you've taken me?"

"Goddamn I want to, but you're keeping me at arm's length."

Neither of us said any more as our food was brought out. I could barely hold my fork straight as I ate.

"It's good."

That was all I could say.

## DECLAN

My driver brought us back to her office building, and for the duration of the trip, our hands kept bumping into each other accidentally. It was as though they were being drawn together like magnets. When the car came to a stop, I didn't want her to get out.

She opened the door without glancing at me, but before she got out, she stopped. Turning back to me, her lips crashed onto mine. I wasn't sure if was a dream or not, but I wasn't letting her go. I pulled her closer to me and her lips parted for me to taste her. Her hands pulled on my hair, as mine cupped her breasts through her dress.

When I reached for her zipper, she stopped and pulled away from me.

*No!*

"Goodbye, Declan. You are now my client and I won't fuck my clients. So stop tempting me," she whispered, her lips inches from me. She moved to kiss me again, but stopped herself and broke free from my grasp.

"God fucking damn it!" I hissed in frustration when the door closed. I was so hard that it hurt.

"Where to——?"

"Where do you think? Home!" I replied as I leaned back and closed my eyes. I wanted to take a cold shower....no, I wanted to get myself off while I thought about her *before* I took a cold shower.

Feeling my phone, I grabbed it without checking who was.

"What?" I snapped.

"Declan."

I sat up as I recognized my uncle's voice.

"Sedric. Sorry——"

"What's the matter with you lately?"

"I took the woman he was lusting over and now he's bitching like a little girl," Liam lied and I realized that this was a conference as Neal snickered in response.

"Get over it," Sedric said seriously.

"I already have. You know how Liam likes to brag."

"Hey——"

"The club owner," Sedric cut him off, his voice stern and low. I could hear him flipping through something. This was business.

"Yeah. He was in a coma. I guess we were a little too rough." Liam snickered. Though Liam had been the one to take care of it all.

"He's awake and I want you to burn down his club," Sedric said before Liam could say anything else. "I heard he had a business partner. Make sure he can't stand on his legs either."

"Understood. Is Otis talking?" I asked.

"All of you need to be on the lookout. A new gang is in the city. They call themselves the Seven Bloods. We've lost a lot of cocaine about the same time they started selling theirs. It's a perfect match to ours."

"A gang did this?" Neal finally chimed in.

"We were all gangs once. They aren't any different. Not only do they not respect us, they are far more organized than they let on. The Ram is one of their houses."

"Are you sure we shouldn't just kill them?" Liam questioned.

There was a pause for a moment. "Declan, go the hospital tonight and see if you can get more out of Otis. If not, then do what you need to do. Neal and Liam, I want you to head to the club tonight. I already have cars for you to switch with before you go."

He hung up.

"Have either of you heard of the Seven Bloods?" Neal asked.

"No," Liam answered before hanging up on Neal.

"I'm sick of my father making me go on these *brotherly* assignments with him."

"Well, if either of you fuck up, it will be your last assignment, that's for sure."

If there was one thing Sedric Callahan didn't tolerate, it was a mistake.

I hung up before Neal could bitch at me.

# FOUR

"You don't find love, it finds you. It's got a little bit to do with destiny, fate, and what's written in the stars.

—Anais Nin

## CORALINE

On the car ride home I tried not to think of him, but I turned on my phone anyway hoping that he had called or texted even though I had once again pushed him away. However, instead of seeing anything from him, I had forty missed calls from Imani. *Shit.* I had turned off my phone because none of them ever called, especially if they still had money in their accounts. In the four years I was away I don't think I had ever gotten a call from them for any other reason.

*She's okay, right? Uncle Adam was just in my office this morning; he would have said something…*

Dialing, I called her back.

"Where are you? I called you like million times!" she yelled and then broke out into a fit of sobs.

"Imani…"

"Cora." She sobbed.

"Imani? Are you okay? What is it?"

"Otis got in a fight at the club and he's beat up really badly and ended up in the hospital. They had to put him in a coma."

"Oh my God, I am so sorry! What do you need me to do?"

"Can you come here? I can't see him alone, they're waking

him up now. What if he doesn't remember me or something?!"

"Imani, breathe, okay? This isn't a Lifetime movie, he will remember you. Which hospital are you in? I'll be right there."

"Mercy. Do you remember how to get here?"

"Yeah. I'll be right there, okay?"

I didn't know Otis very well, but what kind of monster would hurt someone to the point where they needed to be placed into a medically induced coma, for God's sake?

## DECLAN

The hospital wasn't that far from me and I wanted to go alone. But Sedric demanded that I have back up. Usually he left things like this to our people to handle. The fact that he had called on us meant that he saw the Seven Bloods as a real threat, and that he wanted them out of his city as soon as possible. I had changed into all black, and was now riding my motorcycle. I gripped on tightly as I sped down the street, cutting off more than two cars off before entering the hospital parking lot. I found a parking spot and pulled off my helmet. Eric and Patrick were already there. They handed me a gun and I glanced at it before I shook my head.

"The sensors are off," he stated.

"No. You two carry. I doubt a gun will scare him. He knows I can't just shoot him here. I'll have to be more...creative." I adjusted my gloves and stepped off my bike.

Patrick nodded as we turned to walk inside. "I heard most of the crew left him last night. He only has a few friends around him right now. If there's any trouble, we have people here."

I paused once we got to his floor. "Well then, why don't we make some new friends?"

One of the nurses at the station tried to stop me from going in. Eric spoke to her and without any further questions, we went up the elevator. I hated hospitals. It brought back too memories for me, but I was sure that that was why Sedric had sent me here—to make sure I could work in a place I hated and still keep a clear head.

When we opened door, we found that the place was eerily quiet; the nurses all drifted around like ghosts.

"That one," Eric whispered as he pointed to the room, and I walked on and pushed through the opening of the door.

Otis lay on the bed with his hand in a cast, his face a swollen mess, and a small woman who sat beside him crying. However, neither of them caught my attention. It was Coraline who stood just off to the side, still in that goddamn dress from this afternoon, who surprised me. Her mouth dropped open when she saw me and I was sure that if this were any other place and any other time, I would have shared her astonishment.

However, I ignored her and focused on the man in the bed.

"Hello, Otis," I said as I walked over to the foot of his bed.

"You two know each other?" The small woman beside him wiped her eyes.

"We go away back. Don't we, Otis? You ladies mind if I talk to my friend in private? I really want to know who did this to him." I forced myself to stay focused on the man in front of me.

"Babe, go," he whispered to the girl beside him.

She looked between us oddly.

"Babe," he said more sternly.

"Imani, come on, let's get you something to eat," Coraline said as she came up beside me, and I wished I could reach out and touch her.

I ignored the urge to look at her as she and her friend left.

"What do you want, Callahan?" Otis asked me. "Breaking my bones wasn't enough for you people?"

"Are you bitching at me right now? Should I feel bad for the fucking moron who thought he could disrespect my family's name? You're lucky bones can heal. If it were me, I would have taken your tongue." I replied as I grabbed the IV and wrapped it around his neck.

"Agh—" he tried to scream, but I pulled tighter causing him to claw at my hands.

"I'm going to say this once. You have two choices—work for us, or die for them. And remember, if you make the wrong choice, death will come for you in small, painful doses," I hissed.

I released the line just slightly, but he wasted his words.

"The Seven Bloods will kill me."

I strangled him again and he gasped as his body rose from the bed.

"Long before the Seven Bloods, and long after your pitiful little rats kill themselves, our family, *our people,* will still motherfucking be here. So again, choose wisely, because as we speak, your club is being burned to the ground."

His eyes widened as he glared at me. "What do you want?"

"The drugs," I hissed. "Where did you get them?"

"I don't—"

"What do you think will snap first, this line or your windpipe?"

"Please…"

"Talk." I lifted his head up and pulled tight before I allowed the line to go slack.

"There is a man. He's from Mexico. I don't know his name, but I will get it, I swear. I'll get it when I'm out tomorrow."

"We will be in contact. Until then, rest up. I wonder how they feel having a wounded dog in the house," I said as I released him completely. He coughed as his good hand reached up to his neck.

"How are you involved with Coraline Wilson?"

He raised his eyebrow at me, confused. "You mean the bitch with the stick up her ass? She ain't got nothing to do with us. I'm only with her cousin because she said she could help us clean some of our money though her Uncle's bank."

"The Seven Bloods are keeping money at WIB? And here I thought you would be useless," I said emotionlessly, before I kicked his broken arm.

"What the fuck?!" he cried out as he cradled it against his chest.

"Don't refer to women as *bitches* in front me or I will kill you," I sneered as I walked to the door.

Eric stood waiting, keeping Otis' girlfriend at bay. Walking around her, I stopped in front of Coraline.

"Stay away from him, and if you care about your cousin, make sure she stays away too." That was all I'd planned to say to her. I couldn't...this was too close. I hadn't thought these two parts of my life would collide like this. It was a wake-up call. I wasn't just a guy...even though she made me feel like one. I was a Callahan, and Callahans were monsters in suits.

"Declan?" she called after me.

And I could hear her heels as she followed me towards the elevator.

"What are you talking about? What's wrong with Otis?"

"Just trust me—"

"Well, I don't. If something's going on please tell me. Do you know the man who did this? How serious is this?" she said when the elevator doors opened.

*The man who did this was my cousin, and the man who would do worse was me.*

I wanted her. I wanted her badly, but I couldn't...what if she saw me doing something even worse or what if she got involved. What if my worlds collided again when she was around?

"Never mind, Coraline." I sighed as I stepped into the elevator. I shouldn't have said anything to begin with.

"Declan, why are you being so cold right now?" She frowned, confused. "You're like a totally different person."

*Because right now I wasn't me; I was the person the family needed me to be. But I couldn't tell her that.*

"Coraline, you've rejected me three times in the last week. I'm not going to keep chasing after you. Please step aside, it's been a long day." The doors closed on her and I felt both relieved and disappointed as I leaned against the wall. But then the doors reopened, and as her hand remained on the button, her eyes focused on me.

*Coraline, no, keep pushing me away, you're right, your instincts are right, I will hurt you.*

"I'm leaving too," she lied as her feet crossed over the line toward me.

*Fuck.* I was goner. Having her this close to me in an empty elevator, I couldn't take it.

I grabbed her and pinned her up against the wall.

"You shouldn't have opened the doors."

"But I did." Her brown eyes searched mine.

My eyes fell on her lips. "You should stay away from Otis. Because he has bad friends." *And I'm the worse one of all.*

"Okay?" She still looked confused.

"If I kissed you right now, what would you do?" I whispered.

"Kiss you back."

"I know. But what would you do after we break away. Run

again? Like I said, you don't know what you want and I'm not going to let you keep messing with me."

I stepped out of the elevator, and for some reason, I felt like I couldn't breathe, like she had literally been so close to me, she'd stolen the air from my lungs. I had told her the truth, but I'd also lied. I *wanted* to keep chasing after her. But reality was starting to kick in, and the magic was disappearing. Her standing next to Otis as a friend when I came thinking I might just have to end his life…it'd been too close.

I made it outside when my phone rang.

"Declan," I muttered without bothering to check the caller ID.

"I'll stay away from Otis," she whispered into the phone and I turned back to find her still inside the entrance of the hospital staring back me. "I don't have a boyfriend, a fiancé, or a husband. I had my heart broken by a smooth talking playboy once before. So I'm a little jaded. I don't want be just another girl you screw around with or screw over. That's why I've been pushing you away, but I really do like you."

*Walk away, Declan.*

"What do I have to do?" I said instead, and it was like my mind and heart had officially declared war on each other.

"I don't know?"

"Why don't we get out of here and find out?" I felt like I could think better if I didn't have to think about the worst part of me…or maybe I was trying to not think at all.

"You lead, I'll follow." She stepped towards me.

"No." I shook my head as I moved towards her. "You're the one doing the leading. It's been like that from day one."

"Well, take over then," she said right in front of me as she hung up.

"With pleasure."

# CORALINE

"You can open your eyes now."

"Did we stop?" I was too afraid to look, and my grip on him tightened.

I could feel his chest moving up and down in front of me, and I knew he was silently laughing. We'd taken his motorcycle instead of my car. I wanted to fight him on the matter since I was still in a dress, but he reached over, hiked it up, and reassured me that I would be fine. Luckily, I was able to change out of my heels and into the flats I kept in my car.

Peeking out, I noticed he had stopped and where now at the Navy Pier. He stepped off first and I as quickly and gracefully as I could, I swept my legs over, closing them shut when they were on the other side. He smiled as he offered me his hand.

Taking it, he led us over to the Ferris wheel that lit up the night's sky.

"Declan." I gasped when he skipped the line.

"Don't worry about it," he replied as the man behind the machine nodded to him. I felt the need to wave or apologize to the people who were standing in line, but I was in the gondola before I had the chance.

"Callahans make their own rules, remember?" he said as the wheel shifted, allowing the next people who were in line to step into their own gondola.

"Yeah, but people will think that you Callahans are assholes."

He shrugged. "Who cares what other people think? That's the problem with the world, everyone is so worried about what someone, who doesn't even know them, thinks. As long as you don't think I'm an asshole, then I'm fine."

"What makes you think I don't?" I crossed my arms.

"Would you have preferred to come all the way here and wait in line for an hour?"

He had a point and he knew it. I agreed.

"Fine. You're not an asshole to me."

"Perfect. Now tell me about the idiot who broke your heart."

I groaned as I glanced out at the pier. Why had I brought that up? Oh right, I was worried that he would've walked away for good, and I didn't want that.

"Coraline, you said you were jaded, but we all are," he whispered.

"Two years ago, while at Stanford, I met this basketball player, which really should have been the first red flag. I knew he liked to party a lot, but I thought he was different, and I thought we were dating, but as it turns out, he only acted like we were together when we were alone and it was great. But around his friends, or at his games, he acted like I was just another girl he knew. Then the season got really intense. I knew that other girlfriends would sneak to their hotels during away games. So I decided to surprise him."

"And he was with someone else?" he asked like this was the most common story in the world, but then again it felt like it was.

I smiled. "He was with two other girls. I stood there staring in shock before I turned and ran—I'm a runner in case you haven't noticed. He did chase me down an hour later, I'm guessing after he was finished with them. He told me that I was his *long-term chick*, the girl he would bring home to mom and that I shouldn't be bothered by the other girls, that he was just playing around before we got too serious. That's when I punched him and took the bus home. The end."

"Did you love him?" His eyes were soft, and he looked my face over like he was trying to read me.

"Yeah. I think so? I'm not sure. I think I was in love with believing in love."

"So after that, you just cut yourself off from any sort of affection whatsoever?"

I didn't want to go this deep into my emotions.

"You said we're all jaded, so tell me, who hurt you?"

He smiled, and under the light of the Ferris Wheel, he looked sinful and devious.

"I've never been in love before."

"But you said—"

"I said we are all jaded. But not everyone is jaded by love, Coraline. I've never given my heart anyone, which should prove that there is something wrong with me. People should fall in love and deal with heartbreak, I think it's healthy."

"But…"

"But I'm not going to force myself to love anyone or anything. When it happens, it happens."

"Then what makes you jaded?"

"My past. My present. My future."

"Sometimes I feel like you're trying to tell me something without really telling me anything."

He snickered as he pulled off his gloves. "I like you, Coraline. I have no idea why, but I do, and I want to get know you more because I feel like it's happening…at least for me anyway. I'm going on a trip in a couple days, so come with me. And promise to make sure you have fun from the moment we get there."

"Okay."

# FIVE

"And she was terribly aware that she was alive. Not just living and breathing, but ...alive."

—Mary Balogh

# DECLAN

"I would like to remind you that you only met this woman a week ago and you're already bailing out on our plans," Liam said over the phone.

"Aren't you in bed with a model right now?"

"That's beside the point," he said. "We don't ditch each other for women."

"In all honesty, I'm tired of seeing your face, Liam."

"You know what? I hope she breaks your heart into ten thousand pieces."

"I'm hanging up, ass." I hung up before he could reply.

I pulled up in front of the WIB cooperate office just as she came out dressed in a cream-colored jacket, jeans, and flats. I'd offered to pick her up at home, but she said she had a quick errand to run at the office.

"Hey," I said as I stepped out of my car and walked towards her.

"Sorry to make you drive all the way downtown. I didn't want to have to reschedule this."

"It's no problem." I held the door open for her before I headed back over to the driver's seat. "Is everything okay?" I asked her when I sat down.

She nodded. "The WIB is voting on something today, so I had to be there. Don't worry though, your money is safe."

"Glad to hear that. Is this why you studied business? For your father's bank?" I asked.

"Yeah. I used to have so many people try to explain things to me when I was younger, either that or I would have to withdraw my vote for things. My father started this with his own hands. I, at least, wanted to keep it running."

"It's admirable. Most people would just take their cut and not worry much about where it came from."

"I'm not most people."

I looked at her. "No, you are not."

She smiled, as she glanced out the window as the city faded behind us. I stepped on the accelerator, eager to get to the airport so that we could begin our trip.

"Where are we going?"

"To let loose," I replied. "You cleared your week, right?"

"Yeah, but you only said to dress comfortably and bring my passport without packing."

I could tell she was nervous again.

"Do you trust me?" I asked.

"Yes."

"Good. You're taking a calculated risk, and that's when the fun starts," I replied, as I drove towards the private plane.

"What about clothes?"

"We'll buy some when we get there. First lesson, Coraline, don't think about it, just enjoy it," I said, as we came to a stop on the tarmac.

The pilot and our flight attendant stood waiting for us.

"When I said fun, I meant dancing and stuffing our faces with all kinds of different foods," she whispered, as she stared at the plane.

"We're going to do those things, just not in Illinois."

"Welcome aboard, Mr. Callahan," the pilot said.

"Take care of us, Oliver."

"Of course." He followed us inside as we took our seats.

Coraline's eyes glanced over every inch of the jet, from the polished wooden tables, to the tan leather chairs, to the television that hung up two seats behind me.

"There's a bedroom in there if you get…tired."

I waited for her eyes to drift back to me.

"How long are we going to be in the air?

"Not long. Do you want to run before he closes the doors?" I really hoped she didn't.

She grinned. "Would you let me?"

"Would you want to?"

"Mr. Callahan." The flight attendant drew my attention away from her, much to my annoyance. "Would you like anything once we're in the air?"

I thought for a second, my eyes drifting to Coraline as she took off her coat.

"Yes, two large cups of coffee, but fill them up only midway."

"Seriously?" Coraline laughed.

"We never finished our first round, might as well now."

"You don't do anything halfway, do you, Mr. Callahan?" She looked me over carefully.

"When I'm pursuing something I want, I go all out. Life's too short not to."

"And you want me?" It was like she was still trying to make sure, and every time she asked, my conviction became stronger.

"Yes." I wanted her, and for now, that was all that mattered to me.

"You're being reckless, Mr. Callahan," she whispered as we started to taxi down the runaway. She gripped the ends of her seat, but she didn't look away from me. "When you whisk a girl away for a week-long date, she might not let you go."

"That's the plan. I'm looking forward to exploring the world with you. It's going to be just Declan plus Coraline."

"Now I'm excited." She smiled, and thanked the flight attendant as we were handed our cups of coffee.

I couldn't wipe the grin off my face as I watched her. I had racked my brain trying to think of things we could do. Things she would like, but that didn't involve being around too many people, while still getting my other jobs done. As much as Liam bitched, he had actually offered to handle everything back home for me, including keeping an eye on Otis, until I got back. God knew when I would seriously be interested in anyone again. She wasn't around me for the money—she was significantly well-off on her own. She wasn't looking for fame or dying for my attention. She was sweet—she said thank you to everyone around her at least twice, and on top of it all, she was beautiful and intelligent. If she were Irish, I would have already had brought her home to Sedric. We had a rule in our family. Everyone had to be married by their thirtieth birthdays. Because of our lives, it was just easier to marry one of our people...and yet I was here.

"Are you okay?" she asked, as she placed her hand on mine.

I stared at her for a moment, my mind completely blank.

*Why the hell am I acting like this?*

"I'm fine. You should rest now, so you aren't tried."

She made a face and I wanted to laugh at how cute she looked.

"What?"

"I snore and I'd rather you not witness that."

"Do you snore like a cat or drunk trucker?"

"We can't all be perfect," she muttered, not really answering the question as she drank her coffee.

"I'm the furthest thing from perfect." I was a drug dealer, a murderer, and anything else the family needed me to be. My mind screamed that she wouldn't understand, but I kept on pushing forward anyway.

## CORALINE

"Welcome to Mexico. Cancun specifically," Declan said as he held my hand. We stepped out into the heat and I could smell the ocean on the breeze.

I couldn't stop smiling. "Cancun?"

"Yep. Now, let's get started," he said, as he walked down the stairs with me.

A black Range Rover with tinted windows awaited us, and a Mexican man held the back door open, but Declan shook his head as he took the keys and spoke in Spanish to him. Declan's Spanish was so fast and fluent that the little Spanish I remembered from high school was all but useless. The man nodded at whatever he said and pulled out his cellphone.

"Ready?" he asked.

I stared into his green eyes for a second. I wanted to know what he'd said in Spanish, but I decided not to ask. I nodded my head, and allowed him to open the door for me. When he sat down, the driver outside the window nodded to him and gave him a thumbs up. Declan started the engine and we drove away from the jet.

When we got to the main road, it was crowded but I could

still make out two cars, one came in front and the other behind us.

"Security?" I asked looking to him.

He smirked. "You're a smart one, Ms. Wilson."

"I thought it was just Declan plus Coraline? They're making it kind of obvious that we're not just two ordinary people."

"We're two rich foreigners, it's better when it's obvious, *Coraline*. They will bother our security while we enjoy ourselves."

I shifted in my seat as I looked out at the city. No matter where I looked, I could see the pure blue water and white sandy beaches that were dotted with street vendors who were selling everything from bathing suits to ice cream. We passed a fountain where people both young and old danced as water shot up around them. It was paradise.

"Now that we're here, are you going to tell me what we are going to do?" I whispered, unable to shift my eyes away from the view.

"If I tell you, you might chicken out."

"Hey!" I glanced back at him and he was staring me so intensely I fought the urge to look away.

"Hey, what?" he asked, placing his hand on mine. I liked how his fingers gripped onto me.

"I'm a lot braver than I look."

"I'm glad." He focused on the road in front of him.

We drove on in a comfortable silence, while his thumb

rubbed circles on the back of my hand. It felt like he was either trying to calm me or comfort me, and I didn't know why until we pulled into the Sky House. Speechless, I turned to him.

"You're braver than you look, remember?" He smiled as he unbuckled my seatbelt.

*Not that brave.* I was frozen by the time he opened the door for me.

"Trust me."

I didn't really have a choice.

I followed him out.

"Welcome to the Sky House!" That was all I understood from the male and female instructors who met us outside.

"Look up," Declan said, and I could feel every inch of his hard chest behind me. Listening, I looked up just as three tiny people came floating—or tumbling down.

"Second lesson: fun and danger are sometimes synonymous," he whispered, his hands on my shoulders. "I'll be behind you the entire time."

"Let's do it," I replied, even though my heart felt as if it were trying to escape through my chest and my ears were ringing as the blood rushed to my head.

I didn't fight when they ushered us in, strapped our gear onto us, and led us to the small plane, with a rectangular-shaped hole on the side. Climbing inside, Declan turned me around so that I could face him. He brushed my hair back and handed me a hair tie. It took me a second to pull it into a ponytail.

"Good?" I asked him.

"Not yet." He lifted my chin up and kissed me softly. Leaning forward, I kissed him back, and all too soon he pulled away.

"Just in case we don't make it," he said with a large grin on his face.

I smacked his shoulder as I scowled. "We're going to make it! I won't allow otherwise."

"I'm glad to know. You have no reason to be nervous. Now turn around."

When I turned around, he strapped me onto him. Putting on my goggles, I gasped when I felt his hands brush up against my breasts as he pulled the latch down.

"You okay?" he questioned, as he secured the belt that wrapped around my waist.

I nodded, and held on as the plane took off.

I glanced down once as we leveled out to what I could only assume was the dizzying height we were meant to jump from, and I turned my head away. "You should have kissed me way more passionately for a goodbye."

He didn't reply, but I could feel him laughing behind me.

"You guys ready?" the pilot in front of us asked.

"No."

"Yes," Declan said, and we moved closer to the door. "On

the count of five."

I closed my eyes and counted, "1...2...3..."

"Now!" He jumped forward, pushing me out of the plane and taking me with him.

"DECLAN!" I screamed as I felt the rush of wind all around us. But I wasn't brave enough to open my eyes.

*Oh my God. Oh my God.*

"Open your eyes, Coraline!"

"No!"

"Coraline!"

I peeked out and as I saw the blue water, and the shoreline hundreds of feet below us, my eyes opened wider.

"Oh my God!" I screamed and then I laughed.

I wasn't really sure how loud I was screaming or if it bothered him, but I couldn't stop, not because I was scared, but because it felt exhilarating! I never wanted it to end and when we got closer to the ground and he pulled the chute, I was a little disappointed but that took nothing away from how I was feeling. Declan landed us perfectly. His feet touched the ground right before mine did.

The moment I could, I turned around and jumped into his arms, kissing his lips as hard as I could. He arms snaked around me as he lifted me off the ground. Opening my mouth for him, his tongue brushed against my own.

If it weren't for our desperate need for air, I would've never let go.

"Thank you," I said through deep breaths. How I had managed to not have a heart attack was beyond me.

"Are you living yet?" he whispered no more than an inch from my face.

"I can die happy."

He frowned at that. "No, you can't. I have too much to show you."

In one day, Declan Callahan had expanded my world more than I had ever thought possible. I felt like I was alive, every one of my senses were now fully awakened. He'd made me brave enough to jump.

And now that I had, there was no going back.

# DECLAN

I stood on the porch outside our two-bedroom villa overlooking the beach. I'd made sure to have not only clothes brought up for her, but also a personal maid just in case she needed anything while we were here. Glancing down at my hands, I smiled at the memory of her in my arms; how she'd kissed me, how I'd kissed her. She was the only woman I had *dated* since I was a teenager. I didn't kiss women. Allowing them to kiss my body, fine. Fuck them, yes. But I never felt the need to make it any more personal than it had to be. Maybe it was because I had seen how my parents kissed each other as a child. It meant something and I didn't want to waste it, I didn't want it to be meaningless. Liam thought I was insane, but we all had our lines. He never said a woman's name in bed. Neal, before Olivia, never took a woman to any place other than a restaurant on Fifty-Sixth Street. Not once had I ever been tempted to go over my line, and yet from the first moment I met her, I wondered how her lips would feel on mine. And now that I knew, I still wanted more.

*You're losing it, Declan.*

"Declan?"

Turning around, I froze. She stood there dressed in plunge-neck white dress with a thigh-high slit. Which meant I could see her perfectly long legs and smooth thighs, along with the curve of her breasts. She was trying to kill me.

"Shoes or no shoes?" She lifted the heels beside her.

I shook my head. There was no way I was letting anyone else see her tonight.

"Dinner is waiting for us on the beach" I said softly, as I walked towards her. "You look…beyond words, Coraline."

She smiled, crossing one foot over the other as she brushed her hair behind her ears. "Thank you. You don't look half bad yourself."

"Shall we?" I offered her my arm.

Linking arms, I led her towards the stairs, and out of the house. The beach would have been pitch-black, had it not been for the row of lanterns that lit the path and led right to the table in the center. A waiter stood waiting for us and as we approached, he pulled her chair out and seated her.

"Wow," she whispered, glancing up at the stars above us.

"You like?"

"I'm a little past *like* by now."

*Good.*

"You're fine with seafood, right?"

"I love seafood."

Our waiter motioned to the servers who brought out our dishes on silver trays.

"Grilled lobster tail with chive and ricotta gnocchi." He presented the plate to her and she smiled so beautifully.

It was a smile I selfishly wanted to keep for myself, but instead, I thanked the man as he placed my food in front of me.

"What would you like to drink, sir?" he asked.

"Two pomegranate mojito cocktails," I said, and he nodded, walking off. Finally I turned to her and asked, "Why don't you drink?"

"It's not that I don't drink, it's more of I don't like the taste of alcohol." She removed a chunk of the meat from her lobster tail.

"You don't like any alcohol?"

"I know it's weird. In school, there was a lottery going for who could make me a drink I could actually enjoy. But at least I can say I remembered everything that happened while in college." She giggled to herself.

"You're the eternal optimist, aren't you?" I liked that about her.

She nodded. "I'm on the beach in Cancun, eating what I'm sure is the best lobster in the city, with a hot guy who has made it his personal mission to make me have fun. How could I not be optimistic about life?"

I leaned in. "You think I'm hot? I was trying to tone it down."

"Well, you failed tragically," she replied as she took a bite.

"At least I'm not the only one," I said, as my eyes drifted down her neck. "I couldn't think of a word before, but I think *sinful* works now."

"That's exactly what I was going for."

Our eyes met again, and if it wasn't for the waiter who brought over our drinks, I might have cut dinner short. I reached for my ice-cold glass of water and drank deeply in the hopes that it would cool me down enough to make it to the end of dinner.

When her foot brushed against my leg, I jumped slightly and I wanted to both smack and laugh at myself.

"Sorry, my legs are long," she said.

*I'd noticed.* "It's fine."

It wasn't. I was two seconds always from clearing the table and having her for dinner instead.

"You don't seem fine," she said, and once again her foot brushed my leg. This time I reached down and grabbed it.

"Are you tempting me, Coraline?" I asked as my gazed focused on the curve of her lip. She smiled at me under the candlelight.

"I have no idea. I'm following your lead now, remember? What happens next is up to you." She took another small bite.

Letting go of her foot, I stood up and walked over to her. Pulling out her chair, I wiped the food right off the table.

"What are you doing?"

"Leading," I said before I did what I should have done when

114

I first saw her.

I kissed her hard as her body molded itself against mine. My hand slid under the slit of her damn dress and I cupped the round of her ass. Our tongues brushed against each other, allowing me to taste the sweetness of her wet mouth. We bumped into the table, forcing her to let go of my hair.

"Ahh…" She moaned into my mouth as my hand shifted from her ass to cup the warm space between her thighs.

"Declan…" She gasped when our lips broke apart and two of my fingers slipped inside of her. Her eyes closed, her mouth dropped open. "People…watching."

"They'll turn their backs." I bit her neck softly…people were going to have to turn away because there was no way I could make it back to the villa. My dick was so hard it was ready tear a hole in my pants. But her pleasure came before mine.

Dropping to my knees in the sand, my fingers didn't slow down, and my tongue joined them as I licked, sucked, and tasted every inch of her.

"Declan!" She grabbed on to my hair with one hand, the table behind her with the other. Ignoring her, I lifted her leg onto my shoulders. I relished the sounds that rolled off her lips as they mixed with my name. She cried out over and over again and as I tongued fucked her, my fingers thrust faster and faster. She was so wet for me…only me. Her legs trembled beside me, but I didn't stop, I couldn't, even if I wanted to.

"Oh…yes…Declan!" she moaned, riding her orgasm right against my lips.

*It was music to my ears.*

## CORALINE

He licked his lips right in front of me as I gasped for air. My chest rose and fell, and my legs were still spread as he stood into between them. He kissed me, allowing me to taste myself on his lips.

"I want to not just fuck you this time," he whispered when he broke away and rested his forehead against mine. I pulled at his pants, and his dick saluted me the moment it was free.

"Too bad, that's what I wanted." I stroked him...he was thick, hard, and hot. He jerked in my hand.

"Can you tell how much I want you?"

Nodding, I squeezed.

He groaned as he kissed me again, softly this time. "Condoms are in the room."

"I'm on the pill."

"Thank God." He brushed the tip of himself against me, teasing me, but torturing us both. His face was no more than an inch away from mine...He held on to my thigh tightly, and with one hard, thrust forward he was in me and I wrapped arms around his neck as I braced myself.

"Fuck," he hissed. "You're...so...tight."

117

My back arched and he lifted me up as he rammed himself into me deeper and harder.

"God. Please don't stop. Please."

He didn't. His mouth parted and he took me savagely. I enjoyed the wild look on his face. Laying me back down on top of the table, he spread my legs wider and thrust forward so hard that I had to grab my own breasts to keep them still.

"Declan! Yes!" I cried out not caring who heard me.

"You have…no idea…how badly…I've wanted to be…in you again," he said to me between thrusts. "How badly…my cock…missed your pussy."

If I didn't know before, he was certainly making sure that I was aware of it. He wrapped my legs around his waist and lifted my hands above my head with one of his hands, while the other pulled open the cut of my dress, and pulled my bra down. I clenched on to him as I met his every thrust.

He took one of my nipples between his teeth as he fucked me.

"Oh…" I moaned as my eyes closed. My body hummed as he licked around it once more and then bit down hard.

"Declan….AH!" He lifted one of my legs onto his shoulder, and this time when he slammed into me, I came as I called out his name.

"Fuck," he grunted without stopping as he hugged me to him.

I kissed him, and enjoyed how sweet he tasted. His hands shifted once more as he grabbed my ass.

"Harder, Declan," I whispered. And he did. "Fuck me, Declan!"

"Jesus, Cora!" he hissed glancing downwards as his breathing staggered.

"Come inside me, Declan...."

Biting my lip I tried to calm myself down. But I couldn't, his lips were everywhere, and I could feel all of him inside of me, thrusting, forward harder...harder...harder. I knew I wasn't going to be able to walk straight when the sun came up, but I was fine with that if it meant I could have all of this

"God, you're so beautiful," he whispered.

I couldn't speak, each time I tried, a moan burst forth from my lips. He kissed me deeply, as I kept my hands on his chest.

"Declan!" I cried out again.

"Cora!" He grunted, his body shaking as he came.

I could live a hundred years and I knew that I would never get tired of hearing him call my name.

## DECLAN

In the time it took us to recover from our beach escapade and come inside, I was already ready to take her again.

I didn't know what was wrong with me. I wanted to fuck her until the sun came up, and hear it as she cried my name in pleasure. Good God, she was a screamer and it made me so hard. And to think that this was only day one. How would I make it through the week? I could feel myself being pulled in deeper and deeper. I felt like any other human being when I was around her.

"I'm going to take a quick shower." She kissed my cheek and I smacked her ass.

"Go ahead. It's the only break you're going to get from me." I meant it as joke, but the more I thought about it, the more it seemed to be the truth.

She turned around for me and I pulled down her dress. She let it fall to the ground right at my feet, and within seconds, her undergarments joined her dress on the floor. She turned to face me and the moonlight kissed every part of her smooth skin.

My cock hardened and she smiled as she noticed.

*She really was going to kill me.*

"Coraline." I wasn't sure what I was going to say next.

"Yes?"

"Get into the bathroom quickly."

"No." She shook her head.

*Fuck me.*

She took a step forward and placed her hand on my chest. "I don't know what you've done to me, Declan. I used to think I was pretty sweet and innocent."

"And then?" I swallowed as I tried to focus solely on her eyes, but it was worse than looking at her body.

"And then I met you and I become this...overtly sexual woman. I think about how I want you inside of me almost every day now. In that elevator, I wished...God I wished you'd pushed me up against the wall and buried yourself inside of me. I wanted to taste you on my tongue...to feel you in my hands. I'm on fire whenever you're around and I have no idea how to stop."

"Good," I whispered. If she was going to be honest then so was I. "I want to dominate every part of your body, Coraline. I have so many questions I want to ask. Like how deep can my cock can get lost in you? How many times can I make you come in one night? How loud can you get? How rough do you want it? How far do you want go? I want you turned on all the time because I need you at all times."

She kissed me and I just knew that this was going to be a long night.

*** 

*Ringggg.*

*Ringggg.*

*Ringggg.*

Letting go of her, I rolled over and reached for my phone.

*Shit. I had forgotten to call Sedric when I landed.*

Getting out of bed, I grabbed my boxers and slipped outside, making sure to close the door behind me so as to not wake Coraline. I smirked as she automatically reached for the empty space on the bed.

*Ringggg.*

"Sedric!" I said quickly.

"Son."

Though I was really only his nephew, Sedric always called me his son no matter what. I was nine when my parents were murdered, and he took me in. I could still remember being in the car, with my mother's body slumped over and shielding me as the bullets shattered the windows.

Sedric took me home, stripped me down, and washed the blood off of me. It had been eighteen years since I'd lost my parents, and the only reason I didn't call him father was because I didn't want to let go of my parents and he understood that.

"Enjoying your vacation?" he asked me emotionlessly.

"It's not really a vacation, now is it?"

122

"I'm glad I don't have to remind you. The woman you're with, she's not going to be a distraction, is she? The phone rang four times before you answered and you didn't call me when you landed."

"No sir, we're just having fun."

He paused for a moment before speaking. "You've never taken a woman anywhere further than a hotel room, Declan, let alone out of the country."

"Sedric, it means nothing. What did you need me to do?"

"The dealer supplying to Seven Bloods. His name is Emilio Guerra, street name, Slasher. I sent backup down, in case you need it, but I'm not expecting you to need it. Do you understand?"

Meaning he wanted didn't want anyone to know it was us.

"Yes. I'll call in once it's done."

"Be careful, son." He hung up without waiting for me to reply. Like always.

I took a deep breath and turned to go back inside. It was only when I entered our room once more that I realized she hadn't been exaggerating. She really did snore...loudly. But she looked cute.

I walked over and pulled the blanket up and over her since the air conditioning was on. Grabbing my laptop and headphones, I sat beside the dimming light and searched for Emilio. I needed to get away while she was sleeping sometime this week to take care of him. I also needed to send proof to Sedric. He would take me at my word, but I wanted him to know that I could be with her and at the same time make sure that the family work was being taken care of.

# SIX

"Let's take a walk. You can show me some of your memories and I'll show you some of mine."

—Adam Berlin

# DECLAN

It was mid-day on our third day in Cancun, and she held onto my arm as we walked barefoot along the beach. Somehow we found ourselves in the midst of our version of twenty questions.

"What is the best gift you've ever received?" she asked me.

I thought for a moment. "I'd have to say the broken Microsoft computer I got when I was eleven."

"What?"

"Yeah. Liam had broken his, but he put in a wagon, brought it down to my room, and begged me to fix it before his dad found out. I thought he was crazy but he told me that I was good with technology and promised to do my chores for a week."

"You did chores? Didn't you guys have maids or something?" She sounded so amazed.

"Yes, we did. But Sedric, my uncle, said that he didn't want slackers for sons and that our future wives would all blame him for not raising us right. So the maids were instructed to clean everywhere but our rooms. We did our own laundry, vacuumed our own rooms and even had to use the ladder to wash the windows on the outside. Since Neal was the oldest, he usually went up and did it while Liam and I held the bottom of the ladders. I'll never forget when Liam demanded to be paid for all this work. Sedric had everything stripped out of his room and demanded that Liam pay for everything in order to get it all back, plus extra for his 'pain and suffering.' "

She laughed outright and tears built up in the corner of her eyes.

"Oh God, what did he do?"

"Liam's hardheaded. He refused to admit that he was wrong. So instead, he stole Sedric's golf clubs and his wallet, and held it for ransom. Liam got his stuff back but not before getting a few lashes on his arse. So I'm not sure if it was a victory or not."

"What about the computer? Did you fix it?" she question, reminding me of how we'd gotten on this subject to begin with.

"Yep, I fixed it, but not before Sedric came home and found out. He made Liam run fifteen laps around the house and I had to run double that for being an accomplice. But it was a worthwhile experience, after all, it's how I knew I wanted to study computer programing. "

When I looked down at her she was smiling so brightly at me that I almost felt embarrassed. I kissed her forehead, and looked back to see the ocean. It looked like it could go on for miles.

"Next question—"

"Oh no. You've asked me like five questions. Now it's my turn."

"Fine. Ask away."

I nodded as I tried to think of a question that would make her talk just as much as me.

"I know you majored in business, but what was your favorite subject in school? And why?" I added the why part just in case she decided to give me a one worded answer.

"Literature. I would have majored in that, but I settled for it as my minor." She thought for a moment. "I guess the answer to 'why' would be because they're like mini vacations. I can go anywhere and be anyone just by opening a book. It's always so exciting when I start, and so sad when it over."

"What's your favorite book?"

"That's like asking me what my favorite star in the sky is— it's impossible to answer. It changes from day to day. But as of today, it's *PS, I Love You* by Cecelia Ahern. And now that I think about it, the main character, Garry, he's Irish!" She grinned and I laughed.

"What can I say, love, we've been in everyone's fantasy from the dawn of time," I said with an accent and I watched as her grin grew even wider. I loved seeing her smile.

"You're definitely reading to me later," she stated as she nodded her head to herself.

"You brought the book with you?"

"Yeah. Book nerd rule number three: never ever, leave an unfinished book at home."

*She's so cute.*

Taking a break from our walk, we sat down on the sand right at the bank, as the tide brought the water up to just below our toes.

"Okay, next question…"

"Nope. It's mine turn now."

"What?"

She nodded smugly. "See? It goes by quickly."

"Go ahead."

She tapped her finger on her chin and I rolled my eyes as I tapped my hand on my watch.

"When you were younger, what did you want to be when you grew up?"

Without thinking I answered. "Whatever my family needed me to be."

She tilted her head in confusion and I wished I had just said a doctor or something generic…but it was already too late for me to back track.

"You never wanted to be anything for yourself?"

I wasn't sure how to answer this, but I didn't want to lie.

"We Irish are different," I replied. "It's all about the clan, the collective group. When the Irish first came to Chicago, like with Boston, we were treated pretty like much like dogs. I'd dare say only a step above how African Americans were treated in the north at that time. We had no one to turn to, and so we turned

130

to each other. People would have collective dinners for the community if they could afford to, or share blankets or tools if they could spare them. It was your job to support your fellow brother. It was the way Sedric was raised, and it's the way he raised us. That's why we hold a Thanksgiving and Christmas feast in the Irish neighborhoods every year. And also why we have emergency funds if people truly need it. The great thing is the neighborhood's ability to regulate itself. If anyone finds out that you take beyond what you truly need, then you'd be run out of the community." Also, in return for all that, we got their unwavering loyalty.

"Wow," she said softly as she brushed her hair behind her ear. "It's so amazing that you all take care of each other like that. It's like one big family."

"That's the way we see it. Evelyn, my aunt, always makes sure that we have dinner every night together so the inner family stays connected. Honestly, it sometimes feels like I can never get away. Everyone knows everything about you. As a kid, if I lost a tooth, I could walk into Sedric's office and he would be surrounded by extended family I didn't even know, and they would all congratulate me and warn me to not get any cavities on my permanent teeth." It used to annoy me so much when I was a kid, but now I'm used to it."

She frowned as her eyes glazed over. "I'm jealous."

"What?"

She nodded. "My parents died when I was twelve, and for the first two weeks, everyone was hovering around me, so it didn't really hit me until they all went back to their lives and I was left all alone. I had my aunt and uncle along with my cousin. But it wasn't the same. My mother was only able to have me, and so she and my father basically smothered me to death with affection. They went to Greece for a second honeymoon and I told them that I would be fine. But they still called twice a day every day while they were gone. And on the day they came back, it was at three in the morning and my mother ran to my room and jumped up onto my bed."

I enjoyed watching how she spoke while her hands gesticulated and her face beamed with joy.

"She shook me." She stretched out her hand like she was shaking someone in bed. "All the while saying 'Cora, wake up, we're moving to Greece.'" She laughed and shook her head. "My father came in behind her and told her to hush and leave me alone. But she ignored him and kept shaking me. 'We're moving to Greece, Cora. Get excited!' she said again, and my father kept denying it. I was so tired that I buried my head under my covers. My mom hugged me anyway, still ignoring my dad. She talked about how blue the water was, how white sands were, and how great the food was. She talked a lot about the food. My dad said we would go when summer came, but they died in a fire a week later."

She took a deep breath and bit her lips. "Actually, my father died in the fire, while he was trying to get my mother out. My aunt and uncle woke me and my cousin up from our sleepover and rushed us to the house. We got there just as they were wheeling her out, and she was burned so badly that at first I didn't even recognize her. She was rolled past me and her eyes fell on mine as she reached out for me. Instead of going to her, I cowered and screamed. That woman looked like a monster, not my mother. And when they took me to hospital, I refused to see her. She died shortly after, and to this day I still feel like I let her down."

"You were twelve, Cora." I grasped her hand.

She smiled sadly and nodded. "Yeah. I know that, but it doesn't change the way I feel. If I had another chance I would've run to her instead of screamed. If only I'd known—"

"It's impossible to know. It's not fair to be angry at yourself. From what you've said, she loved you a lot. I doubt she would want you to beat yourself up over it." For some reason all the words coming out of my mouth felt like the words Sedric had often told me after I'd lost my parents.

"I know. That's why it felt so horrible when everyone left after the funeral. Everything was silent and I had no one to go to, so I began to set goals for myself. It got me from one day to the next. So I'm jealous of you, Declan. I wish that no one would leave me alone and that at least someone would know when I had cavities." She smiled sadly.

I had never thought of myself as lucky after losing my parents. I never wanted to be a burden to anyone. But I thought about how people were always around me growing up. I never could be sad until I was all alone at night, because that's when I could think again. I hadn't ever been grateful for that distraction from the pain until I'd met her.

"Can I ask you another question?" I asked her.

She nodded quickly. "Please, before I ruin this with morbid conversation."

*What are you doing for the rest of your life?*

"What are you looking for, Coraline? In me, in a man, in anyone?"

She paused. "I don't know, but as the days go by, I'm finding it."

## CORALINE

The way he held me in his arms as we watched the sun set on the beach...I felt at peace. Relaxed. For the first time in my life, I didn't care about anything else. I didn't feel the need to plan out the day or worry about tomorrow, and I wished that this moment would live on to infinity.

"Coraline," he whispered as the sunlight crept downwards below the surface of the sea.

"Yeah?"

"If you ever feel lonely, call me...I'll be there in any way you need me to be. I swear."

I believed him.

# SEVEN

"When he worked, he really worked. But when he played, he really played."

—Dr. Seuss

# CORALINE

The first day we'd gone skydiving.

The second day was bungee jumping and ziplining.

The third was a Mayan cultural day to give the daredevil in me a break. He'd rented a helicopter and flew it *himself* to the Temple of Kukulcan.

The Fourth day we just talked and walked along the beach.

And now, on the fifth day, he was once again trying to kill me.

"Swimming with sharks?! Declan," I said as he put the oxygen tank on my back and handed me the mouthpiece, "you know that this is the reason why women tend to live longer than men, right?"

"I thought it was because you guys ate all that whole grain, gluten free, fat free crap, which might as well not be food anyway!" he joked as he shook his head and zipped up his wetsuit.

"I'm guessing that's a sore spot for you?"

"My cousin, Neal, his wife is all about the free when it comes to her food. She roped my aunt into her health craze last month.

139

So we were all forced to either sneak in meals or just eat out." He'd said it so causally he must have not realized it, but I did. He had starting talking about his family.

"I prefer all the fat in my food. I always figure that I can work it off later. Preferably before becoming food for sharks." I pointed to the steel cage that hung off the corner of his yacht and the crew he had working on it.

"Everyone knows sharks don't like chocolate, you'll be fine."

I stared at him for a second before I broke out into a fit of laughter.

"Is this scientifically proven?"

"Well, we're about to find out." He took my hand, as the crew dipped the cage into the water.

"Wait," I said, as I let his hand go and grabbed my swim cap. There was no way I was going to have time to fix my hair if the water ruined it.

I packed it in as best as I could and turned to find him looking at me with his eyebrow raised.

"I look so sexy right now, don't I?" I posed for him.

A grin spread across his face as he pulled me close. His held on to my hand just before we jumped into the water. Slipping the goggles over my eyes, he made sure my oxygen was secure and working before he tested his. He gave them a thumbs up to the crew above us and once the cage was lowered, I gripped onto him for dear life.

The lights came on and I took calm breaths like he'd instructed me to. When I looked up I could see the bottom of the boat a few feet above us, and it only took a second before not one or two, but a shitload of sharks came out of nowhere and began circling us. It was like a horror show.

I glanced to Declan and he was watching me closely, only allowing his right hand to float out the cage and grace the top of one of the sharks.

He took my hand and slowly poked it out of the bars as well. With his hand on mine, I was able to touch the sharks as well.

Five days into our trip and I was unable to stop smiling.

Was there anything he *couldn't* do?

He pulled out the camera and positioned me in front of one of the sharks. I wasn't sure what else to do, so I threw up a peace sign at the lens. He took the picture while shaking his head at me. I swam to him and wrapped my arms around his neck as he held his arm out so that we could take one together. He wrapped his hand around my waist and lifted me up higher so our faces were side by side before taking the picture.

We stayed down there for only a few minutes before the cage began to make its way back up.

When we broke the surface, I took off my goggles. "Are you afraid of anything?" I asked as I wiped my face.

"What?" He took off his mask and shook the water from his hair before he ran his hands through it.

"I asked if you were afraid of anything. Because from where I'm standing, you're a little too good to be true, Declan Callahan."

"Yeah. I'm pretty much perfect. What can I say," he said as he helped me onto the boat. When I got on board, I pulled off my cap and turned to him. He zipped down his wetsuit and I couldn't tear my eyes away from his abs as the water and sunlight reflected off its hard surface. My gaze followed the droplet of water that slowly dripped down his chest before it disappeared into...

"Like what you see?" he asked when I met his green eyes again.

I shrugged. "You're alright, I guess."

"Really? Okay then." He nodded and I was already used to that look.

"Declan..."

It was too late. He picked me up and threw me over his shoulder, taking us both up the stairs and onto the top deck.

"We just got out of the ocean. I need to shower!" I said, knowing that that wouldn't slow him down.

"That's fine." He led me into his private bathroom, which was decorated in tones of rich, warm, golden browns, all of which were offset and accentuated by a bright white rug on the floor. He placed me down onto the lush rug, and turned on the shower. Facing me again, he unzipped my suit much slower than he needed to. When the zipper was fully down, he peeled the suit off of my shoulder and bent down to lightly kiss my skin. Then he set to work on the top part of my halter-top bikini.

I tried to catch it when it fell, but he grabbed my hands, and shook his head. Holding on to my arms, he lifted them above my head and then grabbed my suit, which still clung around my waist. He pulled it, and my bottoms, to the ground in one smooth motion.

He quickly peeled his suit completely off as well, and much to my delight, I found that his cock was already swollen, hard, and twitching with excitement.

"What next?" I asked him, still slightly embarrassed at being naked. However, whenever he looked at me, stared at me, like I was the only person in the world, I felt beautiful...sexy even.

"I fuck you," he said as he grabbed on to my breasts, and his thumb brushed against my nipples. "I fuck you until you can't stand straight."

"Oh—"

He didn't let me even get a word in before his lips were on mine. His hands gripped my thighs, and he lifted me up around him and walked into the shower.

My hands snaked around his neck and I shivered as I felt not only the warm water pour over both of us and the also the cold glass of the shower as he pressed me up against it. He kissed the side of my jaw and trailed down my neck. His grip on my thighs loosened until my feet were on the ground near his. Then, he flipped me around so that my breasts were pressed up against the glass and he was pressed up against my back. His hands were on either side of my head as he braced himself.

We couldn't get enough of each other.

# DECLAN

I was selfish.

But I knew that already. I just didn't realize how selfish I truly was until I met her. I wanted all of her and by God, I was going to have her one thrust at a time.

"…Declan." She moaned when I slowly entered her from behind, as my hand slipped down to her breasts, where I pinched and pulled on her nipples.

Our days were divided between her exploring the world and me exploring her body in every fucking humanly way possible. I wanted her body to only know me…to fit only me.

"Fuck," I hissed as I held on to her. I pulled out almost all the way before…

*SLAM.*

"Ahh!" She shivered, completely unaware of how sensual she looked with her eyes closed, her mouth slightly parted, as the water dripping down her face and back. Releasing her breasts, my fingers drifted up her neck as I held on to her and buried myself inside of her.

*SLAM.*

"Open your eyes." I bit her ear.

145

She didn't listen to me, as the waves of pleasure enveloped her body. Pleasure that made her toes curl, her mouth water, and her eyes roll back. Pleasure that I had given her.

"Coraline," I said softly. My hand rubbed her ass as I bent her over even more.

*SLAP*

"Now."

Her brown eyes opened slowly, and her heavy breathing caused her breasts to rise and fall.

"Good girl."

*SLAM*

"Declan."

I savored each of her moans as I kissed her ear.

"How many times do you want to come, Coraline?"

*SLAM.* I thrust deeper.

"One?"

*SLAM.* Harder.

"Two?"

"Fuck." She reached back and gripped my hair.

*SLAM.* I moved faster.

"That's not an answer."

"Declan!"

I grinned. "Now that's an answer."

I was already at the edge, but I wouldn't stop until she came at least twice. Pulling out of her, I turned her back around, lifted

146

her up, and thrust into her with no forgiveness.

"Jesus!" Her mouth dropped open.

"Has nothing to do with this." I bit her bottom lip hard, and when I let go, she kissed me back, and her tongue brushed and swirled over mine.

She placed her hands on my shoulders balancing herself.

"Do you hear yourself? This is what an amazing fuck sounds like," I whispered as my face hovered over hers, and my dick slammed into her wet pussy so hard that I was surprised the glass didn't break under the force of my thrusting.

"Yes!" she cried out as her nails dug into me. "Please don't stop!"

"Mine," I grunted. "You are mine."

"Yours," she repeated as she matched each thrust.

"What was that?"

"Yours! I'm fucking yours! Yes!" she screamed and grabbed her own breasts as she came for the second time.

Her voice, her body, it drove me fucking insane. Hugging her close to me, I kissed her hard against the glass, as I thrust forward once more, then held her still as I came.

"God, Cora," I gasped. My vision was slightly blurred.

"He has nothing to do with this," she whispered.

Smiling, I pulled out slowly, but I didn't give her any room to escape me as I stood directly under the shower. The water was now running cold, but I didn't mind as my body was on fire.

Opening my eyes, she rested against the glass...thoroughly fucked and beautiful. She stayed there for a second before she turned and grabbed the soap. Stepping towards me, I realized that her intent wasn't to wash herself, but to wash me.

Taking the soap from her hands, I rubbed it against her body, spending more time then I needed to on her breasts. I wanted ten minutes to pass by quickly so that I could take her again...and maybe one more time after that for good measure.

"What am I going to do with you, Coraline?" I asked as the water rinsed us both.

"Fascinate me. Feed me. Fuck me," she replied. "Basically everything you've been doing."

"I can do that," I said, as I flicked the water off of my face and hair before I turned off the water. Taking her hand, I pulled her to me and kissed her forehead before I led her out of the shower.

As we wrapped ourselves in towels, we moved into the master bedroom. I could see from the window that we were already at the dock.

I still had work I needed to do, and it couldn't wait for sunset.

"Cora." I turned back to find her searching through the bag she'd packed before we left the villa.

"Yes?"

"I'm going run into town to drop something off for my uncle. Do you want to wait here or would you prefer to go into town and shop?"

"Shop." She grinned.

And I nodded as I reached for my wallet.

"Declan, it's okay, I have—"

"My card is already out." I took her hand and placed it into her palm. "So accept it. Besides, whatever clothes you buy, you'll be wearing it for me anyway."

"Fine," she said with a sigh as she shook her head.

"Do you want me walk with you?" I asked as I slid into a pair of jeans and grabbed a black shirt.

She shook her head, and lifted up a blowdryer and flat iron. "I don't want to make you wait. I wouldn't be surprised if you came back before I finished getting ready. Go ahead, I'll be fine."

I didn't like just leaving her, but I didn't have a choice.

"I'll have two men here, Eric and Patrick. They'll take you into the city, and back to the villa."

She placed her hand on my face. "Declan, I'll be fine. Besides, you brought way more security than we needed. If anyone saw us they'd think you were some sort of big shot drug dealers or something."

"Ha! Yeah." It was all I could think to say. Part of me wanted to ask her *so what if I am?*' But I simply kissed her forehead and walked towards the door. Glancing back, I could see that her attention was already back on her things as she tried to unwind the cord of her blowdryer.

At the bottom of the stairs and at the back of the boat, both Eric and Patrick stood waiting. Eric handed me my jacket, gloves, and a gun, which I quickly placed behind my back and out of sight.

"You two will both be staying here." I took second pair of keys and pulled out my phone.

"What?" Eric questioned.

"I want you both to stay with her and follow her as she goes shopping. Watch over her while I take care of business, and remember—she's the woman in my bed, while you're the men on my family's payroll. The order of importance should be clear. Do you understand me?"

They both nodded.

Patrick spoke out when I climbed out of the boat and onto the docks.

"Are you going to do this alone?"

"I have a lot more friends in Cancun than you realize." And where there were friends, there were also enemies. Which was why I needed them with her.

"Check-in in thirty?" Eric asked, and I nodded, already moving towards the old, black Sudan parked behind the Range; I preferred her in that one.

Once I started the engine I dialed the number of my contact. The phone rang exactly three times before he answered.

"Miguel. I'm cashing in a favor."

"After five years?" his husky, voice questioned.

"Were you hoping that I would forget?"

"You Callahans can sure hold grudges. What do you need?"

"It's a skill. I need your boys for a raid."

"It sounds like you're doing me another favor." He coughed, proving that all those damn Cubans were finally killing his lungs.

"When you and your boys arrest them, I want you to leave me half of the drugs and Slasher."

"Declan."

Speeding past the light, I drive further from the coast. "Miguel, how many times has our family helped you snatch the incoming coke from the Giovanni family? Or told you if the Valeros were rolling through?"

"The Giovanni family hasn't come through in four years. Good thing too, I heard Iron Hands has gotten even more merciless over the years. Right before they left Cancun, they gave us a parting present, four of our largest dealers' heads on police cruisers, with *ladrón* carved into their heads."

*Ladrón* …thief. I wondered how much they must have stolen from Orlando Giovanni for him to go that far. Four years ago, they were dying off, begging to make peace with the Irish. Now they were well on their way to being just as strong as us. If Liam didn't marry Orlando's daughter, God only knew how bloody the future would be. The reason why the Seven Bloods and Slasher were now our problem was because the Giovannis had

151

left a void in a prime trade route.

"Either way, Miguel," I said, as I gathered my thoughts. "It's a win-win for both of us. I get a thug, and you get to look like you're cleaning up the streets again."

It was a useless mission. No one could clean up the streets because people didn't want them to be clean.

He sighed. "Where?"

"Cinco Motel, rooms six through nine. How soon can you get here?" I said, as I pulled up and parked only one block away.

"Seven minutes."

"Perfect." I hung up, stepped out of the car, and began making my way over towards the old, grey building with the flickering motel light.

In the parking lot, a few Mexicans were very obviously noticing the out of place white boy as they worked on their cars. Up on the stairs, three of their whores waited, their breasts barely covered in old bikinis, and wearing jean skirts that had so many holes, they shouldn't have even bothered. I knew the men in the parking were watching me.

"Ay, Papi!" Two of the women tugged at my clothes.

"Cuánto cuesta?" I forced myself to smile, asking for the price, as I wrapped my arms around two of them.

They looked at my watch, then my shoes, and I took off my watch.

"Solamente efectivo! Cash, white boy!" one of the men

sitting on the roof of his old black Cadillac in the parking lot demanded.

*God, I hated pimps.*

I looked at the dark haired women to my side.

"Three hundred." She popped her gum. "For one of us."

*Three hundred? What was I getting, the deluxe service?*

I nodded and let go of the other girl before I followed her up to room number five. The moment door closed, she already dropped her skirt.

"You can pay—"

Clasping my hand over her mouth, I held the gun to her skull.

"Don't yell and your brain stays in your head," I said in Spanish. When she struggled, I pushed her up against the door.

"Sweetheart." I held the gun right between her eyebrows as she turned to face me. "I'm giving you a chance here. Don't push it or you will die. If you scream, you will die."

"You got no idea who you're fucking with. I work for Slasher. He ain't gonna let any of his girls get treated like this with—"

"You sure?" I questioned. "You think he would feel that way if I drop a kilo in front him? Or maybe a mil? You aren't a person, you're a machine. You take it up the ass and he gets the bills right out of you. Now you can shut your mouth and wait two more minutes."

"Fuck yo—"

I smacked her over the head with the butt of my gun and she fell to the ground. With a sigh, I picked her up and dumped her on the bed. Dropping three hundred beside her, I glanced at my watch.

*Three.*

*Two.*

*One.*

I heard the sirens followed by the start of engines as the sounds of people running outside the door reached my ears. I opened the door to see a squad coming up the stairs dressed in full riot gear. They rushed past me, as I leaned in the doorframe and saluted them.

Miguel came up last, still as short, round, and tan as ever. He glanced into the room then back at me.

"She's alive. We had a little disagreement about her lifestyle choice. Go on," I said to him.

He shook his head at me and followed his men.

"Room eight!" he yelled back to me. I hated the police, but that didn't mean that they weren't useful.

I moved past them as they pulled thug after and thug out of the rooms, along with their half-dressed hookers. I stepped in front of room number eight and peered inside. One Emilio Guerra, aka Slasher, sat zip-tied to a chair with duct tape over his mouth.

"Emilio!" I called to him as I stepped inside. The two officers

154

who were in the room nodded to me as they left. "You and I need to talk. I got a Seven Blood problem in my city."

He shook his head and glared at me.

I pulled out a knife and held it in my left hand while I weighed my gun in my right.

"Emilio, we can do this clean, or I can be dirty. Believe me when I say that I'd rather not be here right now. But business is business and I will do whatever I need to for however long it takes for me to get what I came for."

He lifted his neck, signaling for me to kill him.

Dirty it was then.

## CORALINE

"Oh my gosh!" I stopped when I saw the white, satin Christian Louboutin crystal-embellished peep-toe slingback sandals that had been brought out on a pair of pillows, as they clearly deserved.

Following them, I stopped when I saw a woman dressed in a blood red dress. Her long wavy back hair shifted to the side, as a white coat hung on her olive skinned shoulders. She wore her gold Cartier Paris sunglasses as she scrolled through her cell phone. She didn't even touch her own feet, as a woman beside her, who could use a nice makeover, kneeled and took off her white Jimmy Choos to grab the Louboutins.

"Stare any longer and you might lose your eyes," the woman said to me, without even looking up from her phone.

"Sorry. I just really like your shoes."

She nodded without speaking.

One of the three guards around her stepped up to me.

"Excuse us, miss," one of them said with a thick Italian accent.

Nodding I backed up.

"They look amazing, good choice. Sorry for bothering you

again," I said to her before I walked away.

Was Cancun really that dangerous? I had asked Eric and Patrick to wait outside, but maybe I shouldn't have.

# EIGHT

"Sometimes we want what we want even if we know it's going to kill us."

—Donna Tartt

## CORALINE

It was our last night here and I hated the thought of leaving. We had spent the day as complete tourists; going through the city, eating from street vendors, and having our portraits drawn by street artists. And for his closing act, Declan was making dinner—chef hat, apron, and all.

"You still haven't told me what you're making." I leaned over the counter, but he closed the lid before I could see.

"I said it was a surprise."

"Aren't you tired of surprising me?"

"Not even a little bit." He blew on the wooden spoon and lifted it to my lips for me to try.

I moaned. God, it was good.

"And here I thought I was the only one who could make you moan like that," he pouted, as he licked the spoon.

"Apparently, it's not just you, but everything involved with you. So far you've proven that you're fearless, bilingual, a master chief, a devil in bed—"

"A devil? Really?" He grinned and wiggled his eyebrows. "I'm honored to have pleased you so well. What put me over the top? The second night I took you from behind? Or was it the fifth day when you rode my tongue—"

"And you are gentleman, for the most part, with a good family," I cut him off without answering.

He snickered to himself, as he turned his attention back to his pots.

"Come on, you've gotten to know some of my flaws. You know I snore, I run away from commitment, I don't drink, I don't party unless I'm dragged out of my house and I don't really have an adventurous bone in my body despite having enough funds and resources to do pretty much whatever I wanted... you're almost too perfect, you must have a flaw of some sort. So tell me, what is it? Are you secretly a serial killer? Do you not want kids? Do you have dirty thoughts about family members or perhaps some weird fetish?"

"The only person in the world who thinks those are flaws is you, Coraline, and that doesn't count. And regarding all of the questions you asked afterward, the answer is no."

"Hey, my flaws are crimes against my twenties, okay?" I replied, and he laughed at me while stirring the vegetables.

"Fine." He sighed as he put the burner on low, and wiped his hands on the dishcloth that was draped over his shoulder.

"Fine?"

He nodded and walked over to me with the same virgin drink we'd had on our first night. Handing it to me, he leaned in.

"I have a fear of clowns."

I stopped and looked him over, his face was serious, but I saw his the corner of his lip twitch.

"You're lying, aren't you?"

He nodded and I lightly smacked him on the shoulder.

"Seriously, what's your biggest flaw, Declan Callahan?"

He thought for a moment, as he leaned against the counter.

"I have nightmares," he said softly. I waited for him to go on. "My parents died in front of me when I was nine, which is why I live with my uncle and his family now. The nightmares were worse when I was younger. I even used to wet the bed too. Now I just wake up shaking and covered in a cold sweat."

"Every night?"

He took my cup and sipped at its contents. "For the most part. I can usually only get a good night sleep after staying up a couple days or pills. But I prefer to stay awake rather than take pills."

"So..." I tried to think back, but each night I usually ended up going to bed before him. "You haven't slept since we've been here?"

"On the contrary, I've never slept better. And it's all because I have you next to me. I haven't even thought of my parents. At home, it's obvious. I love my family, Sedric has always made sure that I knew he thought of me as his son. I told you that before. He even takes me out to Cubs games for father-son bonding. I'm

163

so grateful. But—"

"But he still isn't your dad," I finished for him. "I understand, what were your parents like? Your mother's name was Kelly Laoghaire?"

He nodded. "She grew up in Boston, then moved to Chicago to marry my father, Killian. She'd only met him once when they were teenagers."

"No way? It was an arranged marriage?" People still did that?

He nodded. "My grandfather arranged marriages for both of his sons. He was all about 'keeping it Irish.' "

I frowned at that knowing that if I ever met his grandfather it would be…interesting.

"Don't worry." He kissed my lips softly. "Sedric didn't listen to him either. Evelyn, my aunt, is half Irish, half American. My grandfather almost went insane, trying to get him to marry the woman he chose. But Sedric wouldn't. He married Evelyn the moment they were both legally able to."

"What did you grandfather do?"

He smiled. "He disowned him and cut him off from the family money. It was only after my father died that he was forced to get over it since Sedric had to take over the family business."

"Family business?"

He paused for a second and it was so quick that I wouldn't have even noticed it if it weren't for the fact that he looked like he was kicking himself in the head, as he moved away from me and back around the counter to the stove.

"My family owns shares in many small business all around the country." He stirred the pot.

"If it was so hard back then, how did the Callahans come into money?" I paused thinking more to myself than anything.

He snickered softly. "Fights."

"You're kidding."

He shook his head. "At the very beginning, the Callahan family was nothing bunch of hot blooded Irish men in boxing rings. On our family crest it says; Troid le do lámha, bite le do chuid fiacla, déan cinnte a théann siad a codladh."

I shivered and leaned towards him. He sounded so...exotic when he spoke like that.

"What does that mean?"

"Fight with your hands, bite with your teeth, make sure they go to sleep." He smiled.

"The fighting Irish."

"Damn straight."

I giggled as I shook my head.

"One order of spicy minced beef and pea curry, milady," he stated as he placed the food in front of me.

I looked up at him as he waited for me to pass judgment on his cooking skills. Taking a bite, I said the first and only thing that came to mind. "Wow."

Smiling to himself, he came over and sat beside me. "My aunt would bring chefs to the house for cooking classes when we were younger. She said that every man should know how to cook."

"She's so wise, keep listening to her." I took another bite.

"I'll let her know you think so."

He grabbed the remote and I turned to him. "What?"

"I love this song. I heard it once before, but I haven't been able to find it again."

I put down my spoon and took him by the hand as I led him towards the windows.

"The food—"

"You can't let a good song go to waste," I said as I forced him to dance with me.

He spun me around with ease.

"Great. You can dance too."

"What can I say, I'm almost the perfect man…almost."

*Almost? He was the perfect man.*

We were dancing at first and then both of us just started to sway back and forth on the living room floor. I rested my head on his chest and closed my eyes.

"I don't want to go back tomorrow," I confessed.

"Neither do I."

I smiled. "Run away with me then, this time it will be my treat."

He snickered and kissed the top of my head. "You make a tempting offer. But I can't, my family needs me."

"Yeah, I know." I knew I was going to have to deal with my family again too.

When the song ended, we were still swaying without really caring about what was playing on the radio.

"What do you want to do tonight...?" I drifted off when my stomach growled.

"Well, one of your requirements was to feed you, so let's start with that." He led me back to the kitchen. Grabbing my plate, he covered it before he placed it into the microwave. He only had it in there for a minute before the steaming plate of food was placed in front of me again.

"Step one, done," I said, taking a hot bite. "What else?"

"Tell me more about you."

"More? I'm not sure what more there is left to tell about me."

He nodded as he sat next to me on the bar stool. "What are your hopes and dreams, Coraline? Where do you see yourself in the future?"

"Only if you answer as well."

"Fine by me. But I can't promise to answer everything."

There he went again, pulling me closer while pushing me away. I wasn't sure what he could possibly think was so scary about him.

"Okay, let see. I hope and dream for something more out of life. I'm not sure what it is exactly...I guess I dream about being happy. But then again who doesn't," I said softly.

167

"And what about in the future?"

"Isn't that the same thing?"

He shook his head. "Close your eyes."

I put my fork down and did what he said. It was only when he brushed my hair behind my ears and kissed my shoulder did I realize he was behind me. His chest pressed against my back, as his hands slid to my waist and his mouth barely touched my ear.

"Imagine yourself ten years from now. You wake up, and what's the first thing you see?"

"The sun, it's blinding me, so I turn around and curl up next to..."

"Next to who?"

*Him*, but I didn't want to say that. "I'm not sure."

"What do you do next?"

"I give up on sleep and kiss the man beside me. He smiles and rolls on top of me."

"Do you both fuck or make love?"

"A little of both."

"And when you're done?"

I smiled leaning against his back. "We want to go at it again but our kids start banging on the door."

"Cock blockers," he whispered and I giggled.

"Welcome cock blockers...ahh...the man besides me gets up, and only after we have on our robes, he picks our son and daughter up in his arms. They're laughing their heads off and I can't wipe the smile off of my face. We're going to have a family picnic."

"A picnic?"

"Yes, not just for us, but a whole family picnic. We will dance around a fire pit in the middle of the park while our kids play with their cousins. I'll plan the whole thing." The more I thought about it, the more I wanted it.

"It sounds like the perfect happily ever after."

I stopped, and turned on the stool to face him. "It isn't a happily ever after, it's just the beginning of a new story."

"How do I read it?"

"Just fill in the blanks in your head," I said and reached up to touch his face. He hadn't shaved since he'd gotten here. While I liked the little scruff he had going, I also liked it when he was clean-shaven too. "You said you would shave before we headed back."

He nodded. "My aunt prefers all of us to look *clean and proper.*"

"Let me do it?"

"Later."

And then he kissed me.

## DECLAN

It was midnight and she sat on my lap, her legs on either side of me, dressed only in my shirt. My whole shaving kit was on the table, washcloth, straight razor, and shaving cream. Using the brush, she gently spread it all across my chin and cheeks.

"Hey, head up," she demanded, as she grabbed the razor blade. "You trust me, right?"

"I'll let you know," I lifted my head for her. I had never been shaven by anyone. I preferred to be the only person who held a knife to my throat. But I couldn't say no to her. She was so serious, concentrating only on my skin as she pressed the blade from my neck to the top of my chin slowly.

"You're beautiful," I whispered.

"Don't distract me." She smiled without meeting my gaze.

"Yes, *ma'am.*"

She bit her bottom lip, and I could see myself in her brown eyes.

"Close your eyes. I can feel you burning a hole in the side of my face."

"You're really going to deny me the sight of you?"

"For only for five more minutes."

"Fine," I whined, and as I closed my eyes, I found that I was even more aware of her. She smelled like fresh jasmine.

Our flight was in five hours. I wanted to stay with her longer, but I couldn't. Sedric would want me back before the family went to church. There were two things the Callahan family always did together; dinner and noon mass…

"Done."

I grabbed the hot towel and cleaned the rest of the shaving cream off of me. Opening my eyes, she handed me the mirror.

"What do you think?"

Shifting my head side to side, I touched my smooth skin and smirked. "I might employ you full time."

"Come on, we should go to bed." She stretched out her hand for me.

Taking it, I followed her into the bedroom and allowed her to crawl into bed before I slid in beside her. She rested her head on my chest, as I put my arm around her.

"You never asked me what I hoped for, or where I saw myself in ten years," I whispered, staring up at the ceiling.

"You distract me too easily," she said as she yawned, "tell me in the morning."

I waited a few minutes, and sure enough she started to snore, but I had gotten used to it…funny enough it made me feel comfortable that she could sleep so well in my arms.

"I try not to think of the future," I whispered. "In my life I'm not sure what will happen tomorrow or if we will even make it to tomorrow. But for now, Cora…I want to be that guy next to you in ten years. You deserve a good man and I'm not good, Cora. I can't change that about myself. But I still want to be that guy next to you in ten years."

These last seven days…they weren't nearly enough. I wanted more.

I was going to hurt her.

She was going hate me.

I knew it. I could see it happening.

But I wanted her anyway.

# NINE

"Love, like fortune, favors the bold."

—E.A. Bucchianeri

## CORALINE

I stared up at the large, white house in front of me with the perfectly trimmed lawn and I wanted to crawl back into his Aston Martin. I already missed the warm Cancun air, the heat of the sun, and the sand under my toes.

"You're coming to mass right?" he asked, drawing my attention away from the house in front of me.

Glancing at my watch it was only ten a.m., which meant I had more than enough time to get ready. "Yeah. We made it back faster than I thought."

"Good. I can't wait to feed you again."

"Declan!"

"Feed you the host, Coraline." He laughed at me and I knew he held back on purpose.

"You can't make church dirty, Declan."

"Of course I can't, the Bible already did that."

I shook my head at him. "I'll see you—"

"I'll pick you up?" He stuffed his hands in his pockets and it was the first time I had ever seen him look a little nervous.

"What happened to just one week?"

"You don't want me to?"

"No. I *really* want to, but…" I wanted to know what was happening between us.

"Okay then, I'll pick you up at eleven thirty. We can go to lunch afterward. Our second official date?"

I nodded and he leaned in and kissed my cheek before he moved over to the driver's side door.

"See you later." I waved.

"Later." He winked getting in.

I watched him drive off before heading inside my house. The very first person coming down the stairs was none other my Aunt Trisha.

"Are you leaving for your trip now?" She yawned and stretched her neck. "We're going to need some money before you go."

Wow.

"Aunty, I already left…I've been gone for a week. I left money for you all before I went."

Her eyes glanced me over once before she turned back up the stairs. "You son of a bitch! Where's the money at, Adam?!"

She yelled so loud I had to plug my ears.

"There ain't no money!" he screamed back down at her.

"You a fucking liar!" She stomped back up the stairs. "What you do with it, huh? You spent it getting your cocked sucked ain't you? Going to the club pretending you some big ass man when you can't do shit."

"Coming from the bitch who's so drunk she ain't even know what day it is…"

"Welcome home, Coraline," I whispered to myself as I headed upstairs to my own room and they continued fighting.

Over the years I had gotten used to it. My aunt would never leave my uncle no matter what he did to her. It was partially because of the money, but mostly because she loved him despite everything. And my uncle…well he had some good traits. I think in some way, he really cared about her…they were so dysfunctional, that they somehow made it work.

"So you're back?" Imani said from the doorway.

I glanced up at her and immediately noticed that her hair was now a light golden color and that the ring curls stopping at her shoulders.

"You noticed I left."

"You left me at my most critical time, how could I not notice?" She frowned as she took a seat on the edge of my bed…of course it had to be about her.

"Can't one person in this family ask me whether or not I had a good time? Or at the very least where I went?!" I buried my face in my pillow. Couldn't someone just care?!

"Fine. Where you did you go?"

I smiled. "Paradise. It was—"

"Ah," she groaned. And when I turned to her she was

picking at a bandage on the back of her neck, and checking it out in my mirror.

"What happened?" I sat up quickly.

"Nothing. I got a tattoo." She smiled as she pulled it off for me to see. It read "7B." It kind of looked like half the wing of a butterfly though. "Did you hear? Otis' club burned down, so he and his partners are building a new one."

*Stay away from him.* Declan's voice spoke in my mind again.

"Imani, what does Otis do?"

"He's a club owner, duh." She rolled her eyes at me as she patted her bandage back into place.

"You said he was from Southbend. How did he get the money to set up a club in downtown Chicago?"

"He's got business partners. Why are you asking so many damn questions?"

"Why are you being so defensive?"

"You know what?" She stood up and glared at me. "Wherever the hell you were, you should have stayed there. No one missed your ass anyway."

She slammed the door on her way out.

"Fine," I whispered as I stood up and headed over to my closet. I knew she would be back. We would go shopping and she would apologize...or at least take back what she'd said.

Grabbing my short lace ivory Prada dress, with the bow in the front, along with a pair of nude pumps, I laid them across my bed and matched them with a simple watch and a pair of earrings before I headed into my bathroom. Turning on the shower, I stripped down and stepped inside. But when I looked at my body now, I couldn't see it the same way I did before...not without seeing...without feeling *him*. His hands gripping on to my thighs. His lips kissing my skin...

"Ah," I moaned as I touched myself the way he touched me. I pinched my nipple to simulate the way he'd bite on it.

Leaning against the door, I wished he was here, thrusting deep into me again, as he whispered how beautiful he thought I was, while I lost myself to pleasure. I could feel him everywhere on my skin. Remembering how on our sixth day together he'd spent the night tracing my body with his lips and tongue. He started at the top of my leg and didn't stop until he'd tasted all of me. By the time his lips met mine, I was so wet as I wrapped my legs around him, but he forced them apart...

*"I've taught you how to fuck.*

*I've taught you how to made love.*

*Now I need to teach you the full extent of foreplay."*

And he did. He teased me to the point of tears, while I melted in his hands.

*"You came here sweet and innocent...you will leave dirty and sinful...I won't stop until you hear me in your dreams, Coraline,"* he whispered behind me, while we were on our knees on top of the bed, as his hand slowly rubbed that sweet spot between my thighs.

179

"Oh God," I moaned as I bit my lips.

*"Just look at you, Coraline."* He snickered as he kissed my ear. *"Your mouth's open, your pussy dripping, just begging me to fuck you. Say it."*

"Fuck me," I whispered.

*"Louder, Coraline. I want everyone to hear you."*

"Fuck me!" I moaned louder as my hand sped up just as his had done.

*"No."*

"Please."

*"No."*

I bit my bottom lip harder as I inserted another finger into myself, while I feverishly palmed my breast.

"Declan!" I gasped out as I opened my eyes to find myself standing alone under the hot shower. Bracing myself against the wall, I breathed in slowly and deeply.

"What have you done to me, Declan?" I whispered to myself.

This was bad. What if I couldn't let him go? I felt like my fate was now in his hands.

But church was a good sign, right? He wanted to be seen with me, right?

I needed to ask him where he saw us going. I needed to know if we were both still playing around or if this was serious. I needed to put my fears aside and be bold.

# DECLAN

She hadn't said much as we drove to St. Peters. Her gaze was transfixed on the window as she focused on anything else but me. I preferred it that way. She had no idea what this meant...how much of a risk I was taking. But I knew myself well enough to know that I couldn't...I wouldn't just say goodbye and let someone else be with her. The thought made my blood boil.

Parking next to Liam's car, I stepped out and walked around to her side and opened the door for her. She stepped out gracefully and took my hand. I tried to lead her into the church but she held me still in front of her.

"Cora?" I looked down at her.

"This was the church my parents attended." She looked up at me. "They got married here. Before I go in with you, I need to know if we are...if we're serious now. I need to know that this isn't just a fling or fun anymore."

She had no idea how serious this was.

"Your mine, Coraline. I'm not letting go until you tell me to, and only when you tell me to," I whispered as I kissed her forehead.

"Don't let me go." She smiled at me, her brown eyes shining as the sunlight shifted.

*I hope she still felt that way later.* Squeezing her hand, I nodded as I led her forward. Two of our family guards at the door glanced at her and then at me before they opened the doors for us.

My heart was racing but I couldn't let anyone know that. The church was packed with Irishmen, both young and old, and their grandmothers too, and I walked in, hand in hand with her, right to the front pew with the rest of my family.

Liam, who sat on the end, was the first to see me. His eyes widened, as they looked at Coraline, and then at me.

He stood up and stepped out, allowing us to step inside. Sedric was standing right there, his eyes as cold as ice. Evelyn stood on his other side, followed by Neal and Olivia. I sat down next to him as Evelyn waved and offered Coraline a slight smile. Coraline nervously returned it before she reached for the booklet in front of us.

"Now or later?" Sedric whispered beside me.

I rose with everyone as the priest came in. "Later."

He nodded and turned his attention to the front. I, on the other hand, turned slightly to watch as a few people pointed to us and whispered…if the Irish were anything, it wasn't discrete. At least Olivia's grandparents were both Irish, it was why her parents understood our family so well. But by walking Coraline to the front row and allowing her to sit down, I had basically just announced that she was mine…she was family. I had brought a complete outsider into our world, and as calm as Sedric was on the outside, I could tell he was fuming.

One of the reasons we came to church wasn't just because it made Evelyn happy, it was for the clan. We wore our thousand dollar suits and drove our expensive cars here to prove that we were able to take care of each other and them. We were the standard, the hope, and the law. Everything we did needed to either make us richer or make us stronger for everyone. But having Coraline just made me happy.

"Are you okay?" she leaned in and whispered, still holding on to the book.

"I'm fine."

For now.

But by the time mass ended I could feel my heart beginning to race as Liam stepped out. I followed him while holding onto Coraline's hand. Sedric and Evelyn walked out of the church first, and the rest of followed. When we were in the lobby area, Evelyn turned back.

"Hi, I'm Evelyn." She hugged her.

"Hi." Coraline giggled as she hugged her back. "I'm Coraline."

"Come, dear, Olivia and I would like to chat with you for a moment. We heard that you stole our Declan for a whole week."

She looked to me and I nodded and smiled as I kissed her cheek.

"I'm heading to the restroom, I'll see you in a few," I said to her and Evelyn's eyebrow raised at me. I kissed her cheek. "Please watch out for her."

She nodded to me and wrapped her arm around Coraline's shoulders.

It was only when they were far away from me that I turned to Sedric who was already walking towards the restroom. Liam and Neal waited for me to follow. I already knew what I was going to say…I just needed to be bold enough say it to the Ceann na Conairte. He wouldn't kill me…I knew that. But her…that was a whole different story.

The moment I got into the bathroom, the back of his fist hit me right across the face.

"Have you lost your goddamn mind?!" he sneered at me while I wiped the blood from my lip.

"Sedric—"

"The very first words out of your mouth should be an apology, not my name, boy."

*Just say it.*

I shook my head. "I'm not apologizing."

"Declan!" Liam grabbed ahold of me but I brushed him off.

"For eighteen years I have been your son, Sedric. Never once have I asked for anything. I have dedicated my life to you, to my cousins, to our family! I have lied. I have stolen. I have killed and tortured, all for the sake of this goddamn family!"

"You have done no more than I, or Liam, or Neal, or anyone else in this family!" he roared, but I didn't back down. I couldn't.

"Well, now I'm asking for something. I'm asking for her. I want her! After just one week. Yes, call me a fool, smack me again if you'd like, do whatever you wish to me, but let me have this one thing. Dad…please just let me just have this one thing," I begged.

His fist clenched and he shook his head. "You've already made your choice…in front of the whole fucking world at that. But you're fooling yourself if you think I have power here. It's now in her hands. When she finds out what you are, what *we* are, and she walks away from you, you will have to be the one that puts a bullet in her skull. Or were you hoping that she would never find out."

"I just need time…"

"For what? For her to love you? Do you think she can love you enough to forget that you're a murderer? It—"

"Evelyn did it for you!" I snapped, knowing that I was pushing my limits. "She was just like Coraline once upon a time, and she stayed by your side."

"And there are days when I wish she hadn't. If you really care about her, let her go, Declan. Let her go before we hurt her."

"I'm too selfish for that."

His jaw clenched. "Tell her. Sooner rather than later so I'll have less of a mess to clean up."

He brushed past me on his way out, and when he was gone, I took a deep breath. Neal patted my shoulder before leaving as well. Liam and I were the only ones left. Walking over to the sink, I grabbed a handful of paper towels and turned on the water.

"Just say it," I said to him as I dabbed at my lip.

"Say what?" He placed his hands in his pockets and leaned against the door.

"What you're thinking. I'm insane, right?"

"That wasn't what I was thinking."

"What then?"

"I might end up marrying an Italian. You're with a black girl. I was thinking, 'when did we become so progressive?' "

Smiling, I gave up and threw the towels into the bin as I looked back at my reflection.

"You think she'll stay?"

"For your sake, I hope she does."

"Why? Aren't you all about marrying Irish?"

He shrugged. "Like you said, for eighteen years you've asked for nothing, except her. Dad's wrong, you've done more than I have. While I was playing around in college you were studying your ass off in computer sciences. Why? Because you thought it would help the family if we had a computer genius on the inside. You have always thought of the family before anything else, even yourself. Now all you want is a woman? I don't care if she's black, purple, green, Irish or not. You should have what you want."

"Thank you." That was all I could say.

He nodded and turned to leave but stopped. "Just tell me, why?"

"She takes away the nightmares. And for the first time in eighteen years I can dream again. She makes me smile a thousand times a day and laugh ten times as much."

"I'm jealous." He smirked.

"I hope you won't always be."

"When are you going to tell her?"

I paused for a second thinking.

"On our third date. I want one more normal day as just Declan."

*Don't let go of me, Coraline.*

# TEN

"I have not broken your heart - you have broken it; and in breaking it, you have broken mine."

—Emily Brontë

## CORALINE

He had asked me to meet him at the same diner we first had coffee in. And I, being the anxious wreck that I was, sped through the rain, just so that I could get there ten minutes early. But much to my dismay, when I got there I could see him already sitting at the window.

The rain poured down and I was under my red umbrella as I made a mad dash from the parking lot to the steps. I was shocked that he hadn't noticed me yet. He was usually always aware of his surroundings. I waved, but he still didn't notice me. He leaned back against the booth of the chair and stared intently at the table. Even as the waitress came over to him, he still didn't move or speak. He was like stone. Walking up the stairs, the bell above the door rung as I entered, and I closed the umbrella and shook the water off of myself. But he still didn't look up. I could see now he was staring at a watch in his hands...something was wrong.

"Declan?"

He blinked a few times and frowned as he glanced up at me and then at his watch.

"You're early."

"Do you want me to leave and come back?" I laughed nervously.

"No." He shook his head and stood up as I slid in across from him.

"Why did you choose here?"

"You don't like it?" He paused before he could sit down. "We can go somewhere else if you like."

"Declan, it's fine. It was just a question. What's the matter with you?" I asked him.

He sighed and finally sat down. Brushing his hands through his hair he looked up at me before looking away. "I need to tell you something and I don't want to."

"Okay…"

"I don't want to because I'm afraid you'll run."

"Let me guess, you're a vampire," I joked, but he didn't crack a smile. "Declan?" I asked, worried now.

He waved over a waitress and said, "I want everyone out, now."

She nodded quickly as she moved over to the other customers, who each gathered their things and left. More than a few of them were disgruntled, but no one could do anything about it as she ushered them out into the rain.

"Do you own the place? You can't just—"

"Coraline." He sighed. "I don't own the diner, but I do own this neighborhood. They know enough to not argue."

"Okay, you're scaring me now," I said softly as he took my hand.

"Ask me why they left?" He frowned squeezing my hand gently.

For some reason I didn't want to.

"Coraline, ask me."

"Why...why did they leave?"

"Because I'm a Callahan, and going against me could cost them their lives."

"What—"

"You were born here, Coraline. You must have heard the stories. The Irish mob owns Chicago. All the drugs and the murders stems from one crime family."

"No." I shook my head. "Declan, what are you saying? Your family has done so much for this city. New playgrounds, rebuilding hospitals, donating food—"

"Just for our image. So that people like you could never believe that it was us. So that you would never think that the same people feeding bread to the homeless are the very ones who are giving them the best heroin at bottom dollar prices."

"Declan, this isn't funny." I pulled my hand away from his.

He stared down at his empty hands and closed them into fists before he looked up at me. "When we were down in Cancun, the day you went shopping, I killed a man by the name of Emilio Guerra—No, I tortured and killed him for stealing cocaine from

193

us, and selling it to a gang called the Seven Bloods of Southbend. Otis is part of that gang. I met you in the hospital that day because I went there to get information from him."

My heart was beating so quickly, as the blood rushed to my head, and everything started to spin. I slid out of the booth slowly. Knocking my umbrella against the ground, I stumbled forward.

He grabbed on to me. "Coraline—"

"Don't touch me!" I pushed him away as hard as I could. I hadn't realized that I was crying until I tried to look at him and he was just a blur. "How could you do this?"

"Coraline—"

"No! You don't come in, sweep a girl off her feet and then, when she's falling for you, tell her that you're not only part of the mafia but that you're also a fucking murderer!" I screamed at him, still unable to believe any of it.

But it made sense.

The money.

The guards he had in Cancun.

The way everyone looked at us when we were at church. I'd thought it was me. But it was him. It all made sense.

"What happens to me?" I froze as my eyes widened. "You just told me the biggest secret in your family closet, so what happens to me?"

"I would never hurt you, Cora," he said as he took another

step towards me. I stepped back.

"But you're not in charge." My hand went to head as I tried to stop the world from spinning. "When we were in Cancun, you said you needed to do an errand for your uncle...your uncle who you went into the bathroom with you yesterday, and you came back with a cut on your lip. You said you'd broken up a fight between your cousins. That was a lie, wasn't it?"

He nodded.

"He hit you because of me. He's the one who's in charge."

Again he nodded.

"What did he say? What happens to me?"

He didn't speak.

"Declan!"

"He told me that you would walk away, and that when that happens he can never trust you."

I laughed just to stop myself from crying. My hand covered my mouth as I backed away from him.

"Coraline, I'd kill myself before I ever hurt you."

"And that would stop him? He's the head of the mafia; if you don't kill me ,I'm sure he'll find someone else. So my options are to be with you or die?"

He closed his eyes and nodded as though it pained him.

"You know, when I met you. I thought I was that I was the luckiest girl in the world. I thought that there was no way a guy like you could be interested in me. Oh my God...I must have looked so dumb." I walked to the door. "I don't know what will happen to me tomorrow, I just know that I can't look at you today." I ran out of the diner and into the rain. I didn't care that my clothes were almost instantly drenched, I just needed to get away from him.

"Coraline, please!" he yelled as he chased after me, but I got into my car as quickly as I could. My hands were shaking as I tried to put the key into the ignition.

"Coraline! Coraline, don't run. Please don't run away from me again." He banged on my window and I made sure all my doors were locked.

"Coraline, I love you!" he yelled and I paused as I looked back up at him

He was completely soaked in the rain that was now coming down even harder. *Like a hail of bullets* my mind mocked.

He kept looking at me....begging me to open the door.

"I know you're scared, I would be too. But you know me, the real me. For a second remember...just remember how amazing it felt to hold on to each other. To make love to each other. Remember that and trust me enough to come back. Give me a chance, *please*. I will never hurt you."

The tears in my eyes burned as I shook my head, even though my hand reached for the door handle.

*I didn't know him.*

*He was a liar.*

"Please stay away from me," I replied as I drove away from him and allowed myself to cry.

## DECLAN

I sat in the diner for three hours hoping she would come back.

She didn't.

So I drove to the bar where Liam was waiting. The place was empty when I got there, with the exception of Liam who sat at the bar with an unopened bottle of brandy in front of him.

"You're going to need your own," I told him as I reached for the bottle and grabbed a glass from behind the counter.

"Someone's going to have to drive your sorry ass home," he whispered drinking water instead.

"I thought brothers never let brothers drink alone." I poured a shot and knocked it back, savoring the way it burned before I poured myself another.

"I make exceptions for the heartbroken."

I tried to smile. "I'm not heartbroken. She meant nothing. I mean how could she? We didn't even know each other for that long."

He glanced around the bar, then at me. "Who are you trying to feed that bullshit to? I don't buy that and neither do you."

"I want to believe it though." Then it wouldn't hurt like this. "Why am I like this?"

"Mom always said when Callahan men fall for a woman, we fall hard and with no reservations."

"She's right again." I smiled as I drank.

"She's always right. It's annoying, isn't it?" He shook his head.

I stared into my glass and took a deep breath. "You remember when you said to stay away from good girls?"

"Don't start listening to me now."

I snorted. "But you were wrong. They don't break us. We break us. By hurting them, we break us."

"Declan—"

"He's going to kill her isn't he? Even if I don't do it he will make sure she dies. He will never trust an outsider enough to let them know our secret."

"Then don't give up on her."

I shook my head. He hadn't seen the way she looked at me. Like I was monster...and I was.

"This is too much. She's scared and I don't want to be selfish any more than I already have been."

Liam patted my shoulder and grinned. "Always be selfish, that's my motto."

# ELEVEN

"Loving you never was an option – it was necessity."

—Unknown

# CORALINE

## DAY 1

It had been twenty-four hours since it felt like my world had imploded. I couldn't bring myself to get out of bed. I couldn't go to work knowing what I knew. Rolling over, I reached for my laptop. Lifting the screen, my email popped up, and the very first thing I saw was a message from him in my inbox.

Slamming the damn thing shut, I turned back around. I lay there for a few minutes, but I felt like it was calling out to me like the One Ring had called to Frodo.

*I need to work. I should just delete it.*

Sitting up, I grabbed my laptop once more and opened it. I tried to delete it as fast as I could, but my eyes were able to read it faster.

*No moment with you was lie.*

*But I'm sorry I didn't tell you the truth. I didn't want to let go of you.*

*Declan A. Callahan.*

*PS—I love you*

It was simple, short, and sweet.

Sweet? He wasn't sweet. He was a murderer. *What the hell is wrong with you, Coraline?*

## DAY 2

*Would you have hated me if I had waited longer? If I would've waited until you felt the same way about me as I do about you, before I told you the truth? I woke up today wondering that. I hope you are alright.*

*Declan Callahan*

*PS—I love you.*

I paused and stared at the screen of my desktop computer in the office.

Swallowing slowly, I rubbed the top of my chest. I wished he would stop. No. What I really wished for was for him to be someone different; to be the man I thought he was.

## DAY 3

"Ms. Wilson?" Constanza came into my office as I stared out at the Chicago landscape. I hated how bright and sunny it was outside today. I felt like it needed to be dark, gloomy, and raining.

*The sun should know when to hide.*

"Ms. Wilson?"

Turning around to her, I watched as she took off her glasses and held them up to the light. Satisfied, she placed it back on her face and looked at me.

"No offense, ma'am, but you don't look well."

I didn't feel well.

"I'm alright, Constanza. What is it?"

"Mr. Stevens wanted to set up a dinner meeting with a client on Friday and wants to know if you're free."

"That's fine, thank you," I muttered as I turned back around and resumed staring out the window. However, before I could allow myself to be lost in my thoughts, my phone buzzed, and once again there was another email from him.

I took a deep breath knowing full well that I shouldn't read it, but I couldn't help myself.

*I'm not poet. I'm not really good at words. The last book I read was a computer programming manual. I have so much I want to say to you. I want to go back to that week. I want to hear you laugh. I want to see you. Hold you. Love you. But most of all, I want you to want the same things. I've never missed anyone as much as I've missed you.*

*That's all I can think to say.*

*Declan.*

*PS—I love you.*

"Why?" I cried as I dropped my head into my lap. Why couldn't he normal? Everything would've been perfect if it wasn't for this one, small thing.

Small? It was the exact opposite of small! His secret, his family's secret, was too big...too wrong. I'd Googled the Irish mob and the things that came up...it scared me. I couldn't imagine Declan like that. He was sweet and kind and funny. I didn't feel alone when I was with him.

Now that he was gone, I felt more alone than I ever had.

*"If you ever feel lonely. Call me…I'll be there in any way you need me to be. I swear,"* I heard him whisper in my mind.

I needed *him* here…my Declan, not some mafia hit man.

## DAY 4

*I think I should apologize for my last couple of emails. If you haven't noticed, I'm selfish, Coraline. I'm horribly selfish, and because of that, I only think about what I want or need. I'm sorry for that. I've lived this life for so long that it's not a big deal to me anymore, it's just what we do. It's who we are, and no one else blinks an eye at it. I can't even imagine what you must be thinking. How scared you must have been when I told you, and how scared you must feel now. This isn't just a small thing, a tiny character flaw. It's huge. It's ugly. And I have to accept that it is part of me. But you don't.*

*I don't want you to be afraid. I want you to smile and laugh and go out. I want you to go to Greece and where ever else you want to go. God, Coraline, I want so much happiness for you that even knowing that it won't be with me is okay because I never deserved you. I knew that but I tried anyway and I hurt you. I'm sorry for that too. The man you wake up next to in ten years should have a normal job…a normal family. Part of me wishes that I could tell him to not fuck up because you really need someone to step up for you. To be everything you ever need.*

*He should take you out at least twice…no,* three *times a week. He should buy you flowers…hell, he should know what type of flowers you like. He should treasure you…worship you, because you honestly are worth that and so much more.*

*I fell in love with you the moment you walked into the Eastside Diner. I was a blubbering fool who I couldn't take his eyes off you. I almost poured a whole can of sugar into my coffee, and stole some kid's umbrella (not my finest moment) just to have an excuse to talk to you. But before I could get the words out, you were gone. I should have known then that you were out of my league. Smart. Beautiful. Funny. Cute. Sexy. Breathtaking...and above all, honest. Who the hell did I think I was to deserve that? A monster should not hang around a queen...he'll forget his place. I'm supposed to be the thing in the shadows, or under the bed. And you, Coraline, shouldn't be with a monster.*

*Thank you for giving me two of my firsts. I'm never going to forget falling for you and I'm so sorry again that I hurt you. You'll be fine. I promise that I won't ever let anyone touch you.*

*Declan.*

*PS I will always love you.*

I sat on my kitchen floor eating ice cream straight out of the carton. I knew I was crying, but I didn't bother to wipe away my tears. I just ate. Sometimes it was okay to cry...

"Can you go somewhere else? I'm having guests over," my aunt said, frowning in disgust. For a split second I moved to get up and then I stopped.

"No."

"What?"

"I'm sitting here until I feel like moving. It's my house, my kitchen, and my ice cream. So take your guests somewhere else…"

"Coraline!" she yelled at me just like when I was a kid.

Ignoring her, I just kept eating.

What I else could I do?

## DAY 5

I rushed into Absolon, already five minutes late for my business dinner with Mr. Stevens, and our client, Mrs. Graham. However, when I got to the table, Mr. Stevens was sitting alone.

"You made it." He stood.

"Yeah, but aren't I late? Where's Mrs. Graham?" I sat down.

"She called to say that she was also running late. Did you read up on her file? She can be quite difficult," he stated.

I nodded as I took a sip of my water. "Yes I did. Don't worry, I'll follow your lead…"

*The last time you followed a man's lead, you got hurt.*

Shaking my head, I took a deep breath as I gripped my phone under the desk. He hadn't sent me an email me today and it bothered me. The more I read his last letter, the more it felt like he was gone. Like he'd let go of me, and it hurt. I didn't understand what I was feeling anymore.

"Before she gets here I wanted to talk to you about something," Mr. Stevens said, pulling me from my thoughts.

Nodding, I gave him my attention. "Please, go on."

"It's about the job you gave your uncle." He frowned.

*Oh no.*

"Has he done something?"

"No," he shook his head. "I checked on him and he's doing fine. But you should be careful. Your father always said that he could never trust his brother. That his greed often gets the best of him. And he's made it clear that he wants the bank. If you aren't careful he could steal it away from under you."

Part of me wanted to say he could take it.

"Thank you…I…" I paused as I saw *him* and his family enter in the restaurant. The hostess led them over to a private table next to the shark tank. I instinctively put my hand up to block my face.

"Coraline?"

"Huh?" I asked as I looked back to Mr. Stevens.

"Are you alright?"

"Tyrone!" Mrs. Graham loudly exclaimed as she came up to us. She was dressed in a full-length fur coat…even though it was summer, and her white hair was immaculately styled and held in place by what I could only assume were a thousand hairpins.

Stevens stood up cheerfully and welcomed her. I glanced to their table hoping that he hadn't noticed us, but he had. His green eyes pierced though me for the longest second of my life before he looked away.

"Mrs. Graham, this is Ms. Coraline Wilson."

"Oh my! You are *beautiful!*" She kissed both of my cheeks.

I smiled. "Thank you so much, you look amazing. Please have a seat."

"Oh, you would never believe the traffic, my driver had to take all the back streets just to get us here." She waved her hands in the air.

"I'm sorry to hear that, ma'am. Would you like to order now?"

"So polite." She laughed.

Well, she could be my grandmother.

"Of course. How else are we supposed to earn your trust?" Stevens laughed, but it was fake and hard to listen to.

They started talking, but once again my eyes drifted to Declan. I noticed how close they were all siting together. Evelyn, smacked one of the boys' hands when he reached for the last piece of bread before taking it for herself. They all laughed...well, all of them but Declan, though he did manage a smile. Another member of their family...Liam, I believe his name was, wrapped his arm around his neck and said something that made the rest of them laugh. Declan just nodded and his eyes drifted back to mine. I reluctantly turned back to Mrs. Graham who was still talking about the traffic.

I couldn't help but wonder how it felt to sit over at that table with them. To laugh, with them like one family. They seemed so happy and warm…was it all an act? If it was, they all deserved awards.

***

When I stepped out of the bathroom stall, there was Evelyn Callahan washing her hands, in her soft, pink lace cocktail dress. She looked in the mirror and smiled.

"Coraline! I had no idea you were here." She turned to me as I moved to wash my hands.

"Hello, Mrs. Callahan." I whispered without looking at her.

"Why are you so stiff? Is everything alright?" she asked so kindly that I had to face her. Her head tilted to the side and her eyes brimmed over with genuine concern as she looked at me.

She had to have known. Surely Declan had told them by now.

"I know," I whispered. "I know who you all really are."

She frowned. "Coraline, that is no reason to go around looking like the sky has fallen."

She couldn't be serious.

"Maybe you didn't hear me. I said I know that—"

"We're the *mafia*," she whispered conspiratorially as leaned into me and a small smile crept over her face. "So? Is that why you're not at my son's side?"

"How can you be—?"

"So what?" she questioned as she turned to look at her reflection in the mirror. She opened her clutch and pulled out a small bottle of lotion. She placed a few dots on her hands before she held the bottle out to me.

I stared at her, too shocked and confused to speak.

She lifted my hands up and placed a squirt of the lotion into them before she put it away. "I swear these bathroom soaps make your hands feel like sandpaper."

"I'm confused," I finally managed to say as I rubbed my hands together. "Why are you like this? How can you be so calm? It's not like he told me that you guys skip taxes, he told me what you *really* do."

"Never skip taxes, sweetie. Uncle Sam forgives no one and has a long memory. You know that's how they got Al Capone, right?"

I felt like someone there should be a sign somewhere saying, *"Welcome to The Twilight Zone."*

"To answer your question." She sighed as she faced me again. "It's not a big deal because it isn't a big deal."

"I'm sure there are plenty of people who would disagree."

She shrugged. "You and I aren't plenty of people. If you didn't know, would you still with be with him?"

I said nothing.

"Of course you would be. You were happy. You, even if you don't want to admit it, already started to picture your life with him. So what? He's not hundred percent good. He's still better than anyone else you will ever find. The men of this family are loyal to the very end. They don't just love their women, they worship them. Anything you could ever want in life, he will not stop until he gives it you. You have no idea how many mothers have come to me asking me to present their daughters to him…how many of them have begged to be in this family. You are always loved. You always have a family. So what if he isn't perfect?"

"The line between a lack of perfection and murder is a big one."

"Then why can't you stop looking at him?" she asked and I realized that she had followed me in here on purpose. "Go back to your mediocrity and your misery, Coraline, if you can't handle the fact that the best things in life always come with a catch. I can see it in your eyes. How lonely you are. It's a shame that you are standing in the way of your own happiness."

She walked around me, her heels clicking on the ground, as she made her way out. I leaned against the counter for a second, breathing deeply when the door opened again and I stood up straighter. But it wasn't her, it was Declan.

His eyes looked over me frantically before he relaxed.

"Thank God. I thought she hurt you," he said softly.

"Evelyn?"

He nodded. "Even I don't know what my aunt is capable of. I don't think anyone but Sedric knows, and if he asked her to hurt you, she would. Sorry for barging in. I just...I just needed to see you were alright. You look nice. Sorry. Ugh. I will go."

He turned to leave.

*Wait!*

But I couldn't bring myself to say it. I let him walk away from me and my heart ached.


## DAY 6

I missed him. No matter how much I didn't want admit it. I missed him, to the point where I almost called.

*Almost.*


## DAY 7

I was at the Elgin Soup Kitchen today. I felt the need to do some good, and feeding the homeless seemed like the only thing I could do. Part of me wanted to remind myself that my problems meant nothing. There were worse things going on in the world and I shouldn't waste my time thinking about him.

"Hello," I said, with a smile, to the small, freckle-faced girl who stood in front of my station of cakes and other breads. "Which one do you want?"

She stood up on her tippy toes, as her eyes looked them all over. Then she glanced to someone who was either her older sister or her really young mother. The girl looked so…broken—and I knew broken. The rings around her eyes told me that she hadn't had a restful night's sleep in weeks. She nodded to the little girl and she pointed to the chocolate covered cake. I gave her the biggest piece.

"Thank you!" She beamed like I had just given her Willy Wonka's Golden ticket.

"You're welcome," I said as she went back to her table.

Next up was rather large muscle man. The hair on his head and eyebrow had been shaved off. He grinned and pointed down to the sponge cake. He looked kind of like a little kid despite his appearance. Laughing to myself, I nodded as I handed it to him. He said 'thank you' in sign language, and I, unsure of how to respond, copied the action. But instead of walking away, his gaze shifted to behind me and I felt someone step up next to me. Turning to look, I found that it was none other than Liam Callahan, dressed in a plain cotton shirt and a pair of jeans. In all of the times I had seen him, this had to have been the most causal. But he didn't look at me. Instead, he started to sign to the man in front us. I looked on as they had what seemed to be a hilarious conversation.

"Any day, Ardal!" Liam said as he waved him off. They clasped hands over the food table before the man finally went to his seat.

Liam grabbed a pair of gloves under the counter and pulled on them on without looking at me.

"Hello," I finally said to him and his green eyes, so much like Declan's, focused in one me.

"Hello, Coraline." He nodded causally before he turned his attention to the next person in line.

A little boy with blond hair.

Liam rolled his eyes. "I don't like this one. NEXT."

"Liam!" I gasped at him and then to the boy who made a face.

"I ain't like your sorry ass either!" The boy said in the strongest accent I had ever heard.

"Listen, kid—"

"*Kid*, I am manlier then your sorry—" Before he could finish another younger boy came over quickly and placed his hand over the boy's mouth.

"Sorry, sir, he's bit stubborn, this one," the older one said.

"You better knock some sense to him." Liam took a random cake and dropped it onto the boy's tray.

The blond boy bit the hand over his mouth and glared at Liam who just glared back to him.

"I don't want this one."

"You know what—"

"Which one did you want?" I cut in quickly.

The boys turned to me and the little boy made puppy dog eyes. "The chocolate one."

"Okay then, let's trade," I said as I handed over the chocolate cake, but the little brat stole it and ran off with them both!

"Tsk tsk." Both Liam and the other boy shook their heads.

"How could you fall for that?" the boy said to me.

"She's still green, Carney. Tell your little brother if he crosses my path again I will hang him up by the ankles."

"I'll send him your way then, sir!" He laughed as he went over to his brother, and put him into a headlock while all the rest of the table laughed.

"So, you come here often?" I whispered handing out the cake.

"One Callahan every Sunday, unless it's my father's turn and then all his sons come with him. After all, it's our soup kitchen."

Shocked, I glanced at him as he handed a piece of vanilla cake to an elder woman.

"You own this soup kitchen?"

"That's what I said. We have others, but this is main one. It's not only open to the Irish either," he stated as he nodded at the Asians who came across to us. He finally faced me. "It seems like you can't get away from us."

"It's hardly fair since you all own everything."

He snickered as he handed the last piece of cake over before he looked around me to the people in charge further up the line.

"Is there more cake?"

"Yeah. In the fridge!"

He nodded and glanced at me. "Come on."

I really didn't want to follow him.

"I'm not going to hurt my brother's girl," he muttered already walking.

"I'm not his girl."

"Why not?"

"First your mother now you. You guys—"

"My mother came to see you?" He frowned as we went into the kitchen.

"You didn't know? Two days ago at Absolon."

He opened the fridge but paused. "Oh, so that's what happened. I knew you were there, but I didn't realize she went to speak with you. I wondered why they both got up like that. What did my mother say? I've always wanted to know what she has to say to the wives."

"I'm not—I'm not anyone's wife."

"Not yet," he replied as he grabbed two trays and headed to the front again.

"You're incredibly—"

"Passionate? Sweet? Oh, I know…sinfully and unbelievably handsome." He lifted his chin in pride as he set the trays down, and took mine from me.

"Pushy."

He snickered.

I noticed that he seemed to know almost everyone's name, not only the Irish, but everyone that walked in, which made me wonder how long people had been coming here. He didn't bring up Declan or anything related to the subject, he just did his job, one of them at any rate, and focused on those in front of him.

After twenty minutes, another pair came over to replace us.

"Which do you want?" Liam asked looking over the cakes.

"Liam, those are for—"

"The hungry, and I'm hungry." He took the two angel cakes along with a spoon and walked over to one of the tables and took a seat. "Come on."

Sighing, I took a seat in front of him.

He slid a cake and the spoon to me.

"What are you going to use...?" I stopped as he picked up the long piece of cake with his hand.

Shaking my head, I tried to think of something to change the subject but I only had one question. "Why haven't you brought up Declan?"

He licked his lips and watched me carefully. "I wanted to see if you cared enough to bring him up first. Good to know you cared about him even a little bit."

"That's not fair."

"When you make a Callahan fall in love and then walk away, *that's* not fair."

I couldn't believe this.

"You all make it seem like I did something wrong. He was perfect and then he threw this…the mafia in the middle," I muttered taking a bite.

"We do a lot of good, Coraline—"

"You also do a lot of bad," I replied as I dropped the spoon and used my hands like him.

"Everyone does bad things. Even you, or at least your company does."

"What?" I snapped as I glared up at him.

He placed his elbows on the table and nodded. "Two days ago, you were at Absolon, eating lobster with Mrs. Lauren Graham, owner of the Graham Steel Mill. The same steel mill that had an explosion four years ago due to poorly maintained and rusting equipment. Despite her workers' protests, she and her board didn't even care. So Ardal over there…" He nodded to the large man that was laughing with a group of other men. "Had the hairs burned off his head and face. He also lost his hearing. So not only does he look 'scary,' but since he can't communicate normally, finding a job, a *good* job, is almost impossible.

"Carney and his little brother, Daly, lost his their father in that same explosion. And instead of compensating the workers and their families, WIB, *your company*, helped her to move her money around so that she was only required to pay out less than one hundred dollars to each family. So congrats, you helped shaft the poor. And my family couldn't do anything but help them rebuild, pay for medical bills, and feed them. But as an orphan yourself, I'm sure you know how little that compensation really means to them. So tell me, who's the villain now?"

I felt sick.

"Should I explain every other horror story here? Would you like to know how many of those *good guys* are on your client list?"

I glanced around the hall, everyone was laughing and cheerful even though most of them had all been screwed over in one way or another. I bit my lip and looked down in shame. How had I not known that?

"Like you said, we do a lot of bad. We sell drugs to people who *want* drugs, and oftentimes, that means our line of work gets messy. But at least when we give back it isn't just for a tax write off." He stood up, but paused. "He gave you his mother's money, right?"

"What?"

"The Laoghaire fortune," he stated.

It took a second longer than it should have for my brain to start working, but I nodded.

"His mother started Elgin in Boston and brought it here. He still has his father's fortune and that was more than enough, but he wasn't sure what to do with it. He'd planned to donate it when we were teenagers. However, it's tradition—should a mother die, her fortune goes to her daughter on her wedding day. Or, if she had no daughter, her son's bride, to do whatever she wished with it."

He left me and went to join in the conversations around the hall.

Once again, my heart burned.

"Lady."

I turned to see the small blond boy, his brother squeezing his shoulder, forcing him to stay still.

"Sorry for stealing the cake." He sighed as he crossed his arms. Then he looked up at his brother. "Happy?"

"Sorry again." The older boy laughed as he dragged his brother away.

*So was I.*

# TWELVE

"The real world is where the monsters are."

—Rick Riordan

## CORALINE

Another week had gone by. Luckily with no more visits from his family.

Two weeks…weeks without him and I was still waiting for it get easier. But every day that went by, I was just a little bit sad that he didn't email me again. Which was crazy. I was the one who'd wanted this and he was only respecting my decision.

*In fact, I needed to just stop thinking about him!*

I came to work and I was home by five. Which meant that for the past two weeks I always had a front row seat to my aunt and uncle fighting, and Imani stumbling inside drunk at four in the morning. I had gone from six places, to what felt like all of the world, back down to one in only a month. It was so insane I could barely believe it either.

*Five.*

*Four.*

*Three.*

*Two.*

*One.*

"Urgh! I think I'm going to be sick." Imani stumbled up the stairs right on cue.

Rising from my bed, I opened my door and went to her. I lifted her up and she threw her arm over my shoulder as I dragged her to her room.

Her mother stepped out and looked at her.

"Look at you. Such a disgrace."

"Takes one to know one!"

"Stop!" I said to them both when my aunt raised her hand to slap Imani across the face. "She's drunk. I'll take care of her."

She didn't say anything more as she went downstairs.

"Bathroom." Imani pushed away from me and ran towards her bathroom.

With a sigh, I followed her inside her pink bathroom, and as I held her hair behind her ears I noticed her tattoo again.

*7B.*

*"Otis is part of a gang called the* Seven Bloods.*"* I tried to shake his voice from my head. But I couldn't ignore what was in front of me.

"Imani? What does your tattoo mean?"

"Coraline, please leave me alone," she whispered as she rested her head against the toilet seat. "Otis dumped me."

"What?"

"Yeah. He said I was too stupid for him."

"He's an ass who wouldn't know a good woman if she fell out of space and right on top of him. You can do much better—
"

"No, I can't," she said as she stood up. "We can't all be like you, Coraline. Go to big fancy schools and live off of the money our smart daddies left for us."

"Why are you taking all your rage out on me?"

"Because you annoy me!" she yelled as she glared at me. "God, you're just so…I can't even! You walk around here like you're better than everyone else, but you know what, Coraline? You aren't. We all preferred it when you were in California. Why'd you bother coming back?"

"Excuse me for hoping my family would miss me."

"There, right there, that's why you piss me off!" she snapped. "We aren't a family! We are four people living in a house. And you walking around taking care of everyone doesn't make anyone feel better. You're like this dumb, little beat-down dog who keeps coming back down. Have some backbone for once in your damn life!"

She tried to grab her purse from the table but I snatched it and dumped everything out.

"What are you doing?"

"Having backbone! This is mine, isn't it?" I snapped, as I marched towards her closet and took back my shoes, bags, and shirts. "And this and this. All of this is fucking mine!"

I threw it onto the ground and glared at her. "You know why I keep coming back, you heartless bitch?! Why I don't kick you and your parents out or cut you all off? Because we're *family*,

227

we're *blood*. That should mean something! We can't choose our family and we shouldn't just abandon them either no matter how disgusting they are!"

"Have fun with all your stuff." She flicked me off as she slammed the door and left. Sitting on the ground, I took a deep breath when I heard the screeching sound of tires.

Standing back up, I glanced outside only to see her pull out of our driveway with my car! *Jesus! She was still drunk!*

"Imani!" I yelled, as I rushed down the stairs, and out the door.

"Imani!" I screamed again when I heard the car screech and a sickening crash as it hit something.

With no shoes on, I took off running down the hill towards the front gate. And as I reached the bottom, I saw that she had driven my car right into Mr. Pierre's guard booth. He lay there in the middle of road, surrounded by splintered bits of wood and bloody shards of glass.

"Oh my God." She stumbled out of the car.

"What did you do?!" I screamed at her as I rushed to Mr. Pierre and searched for a pulse.

"Is…is he dead?" She backed away.

"Call 9-1-1!"

She shook her head.

"Cora…I…I can't."

I stared at her wide-eyed as she ran.

"Imani!" I screamed after her.

"Urrhhh…" Mr. Pierre grumbled.

"Mr. Pierre, it's me. Coraline. Coraline Wilson, help's on its way, just hold on. Okay?" I patted his chest not sure what to do before getting up. I rushed back to my car and pressed the OnStar button.

"This is OnStar, what's your emergency?"

"There's been an accident. I'm at the gate of Raven Hill Heights. I need help!"

"Cor—Cora," Mr. Pierre coughed calling me.

"Please hurry!" I yelled as I rushed back to him and took his hand. "I'm here. Mr. Pierre can you see me? I'm right here."

"My wife…"

"I will call her the moment we get to the hospital, okay? Don't talk right now, I'll talk. I'm good at talking, Mr. Pierre, so just focus on my voice…."

"Jo…hn…" He coughed up more blood and I wiped it off with my sleeve. I tried not to cry as I nodded.

"Okay, John. What do you want to know? I went Cancun, recently. It's just as beautiful as the magazines. You and your wife should go. Women are suckers for sandy white beaches and crystal clear waters. In fact, you have to go, on me."

"Really?" He coughed again, and this time blood came out of his nose. I wiped it away again.

"Yes, really. How long do you want to stay? I think two

229

weeks would do it. One week isn't enough, believe me."

"Okay." He tried to nod as he squeezed my hand tighter.

"Okay then. It's set. I always keep my promises, John, so you've got to make it for me. You and your wife have to go."

He didn't say anything more as an ambulance, along with two police cruisers, drove up.

"Help, please!" I screamed to them. I knew that that was why they were here, but I felt the need to say it again.

"Ma'am, we need you to move aside," the paramedic said, and I moved back slightly without letting go of his hand. "Are you coming with him?"

I nodded and rose as they stabilized him and lifted him up. I noticed the police officers talking to the crowd that had gathered, unbeknownst to me. As I looked around, I noticed Imani standing far off in the distance.

"Ma'am, we need to go."

"Coming." I followed along with them.

*** 

"Oh God!" an older woman with short white hair cried as she fell to the ground. The doctor told her what the paramedics couldn't—that on our way here, Mr. Pierre had died. Just like that, he was gone.

My cousin and I had gotten into a fight and she drove off,

making it not even a mile before killing someone. That was my reality now as I sat in my blood-stained SpongeBob pajamas, unable to leave.

"Ms. Wilson?"

I turned to the officer who'd called my name.

"Yes…yes, that's me."

He looked at me from my bare feet to my hair that was still wrapped in a scarf. "Do you live at Raven Hill?"

"Yes."

"And the Infinity is yours?"

"Yes." I really wanted silence. My head felt like it was going to split open.

"Ma'am, we're going to need you to come down to the station. For more question…"

"Was it you?!"

I jumped at the voice that yelled at me. The old woman, still sobbing, marched up to me as she held on to her husband's personal items.

"Did you kill my John?"

"No!" I said quickly. "Mrs. Pierre—I didn't do this."

She slapped me. "How could you do this to us? He was going to retire! He had a week left!"

"Mom, let's go." Her daughter pulled her away as the officer stepped in between us. I held onto the side of my face, unable to speak. The world was spinning too fast for me.

"Ms. Wilson, you need to come with us…"

"Is she under arrest?"

I turned to find Declan walking up to us. It was six a.m. and he was dressed in jeans and a simple dark blue button down shirt. This was just too much…it had to be a nightmare. Stumbling backwards, I fell onto the chair.

"Mr. Callahan—"

"Is she under arrest, Officer?" he repeated as he stood beside me.

"No, sir, not yet, we just have some questions—"

"Then get away from us. An explanation for this will surely pop up, and when it does, it will come from our lawyer. For now, I think it would be best if you headed back to the station. Your Captain should be calling you shortly." Sure enough his partner came up and motioned for the officer to follow him.

"Have a good day, Mr. Callahan." They nodded to him and when they turned the corner, he sat down.

Neither of us said anything and it bothered me just as much talking would have.

"How did you know I was here?" I whispered.

"One of my men was on his way to drop something off for you. He saw you get into the back of the ambulance and called me. Please tell me that none of that blood belongs to you. Have you seen a doctor?" He reached out to touch me, but then stopped. His hand curled into a fist before he gripped his own

232

knee.

"It's not mine. It was Mr. Pierre's. He died today." I felt like someone else should know that. "He was good man. I didn't know him too well, but he was there at Raven Hill when we first moved in. He remembers everyone's name and always came out of his booth to say good morning or good night to people. He was a good man and he died today."

"Let me take you home."

"Yes, please. My car is the murder weapon." I laughed softly even though it wasn't funny. I placed my hands over my face and tried to stop myself from crying.

"I'll take care of it."

"It wasn't me...It was my cousin," I sobbed as I wiped my nose.

"I will still take care of it, just let me take you home, okay?" He offered me his hand. I took it and held on tightly as he led me out the back of the hospital. Eric was there, and with the snap of Declan's fingers, his coat came right off and was on my shoulders.

"Thank you," I whispered as I sat in the passenger's seat.

He turned on the music and lowered it until it was only a soft hum before we drove off and I rested my head against the window and drew in a shaky breath.

"Is this what your nightmares are like?" I whispered, as I stared out into the city. It seemed as though everyone was only just beginning to get up and move about as they prepared to start a new day. I, on the other hand, just wanted to go to bed.

"Yes," he replied.

"And I won't forget?"

"No. Sometimes we have to pay for other peoples mistakes along with our own."

"Do we ever stop paying?" I looked to him when we reached the stoplight.

He sighed. "You never stop paying, Cora. If you do, it means you're either dead or dying. I never want to see you like this again."

"It's the SpongeBob pants, isn't it? Not doing it for you?"

A grin spread across his lips. "I'm more of Mr. Krabs type of man, I mean what the hell is a sponge doing at the bottom of the sea?"

My giggle turned into a full-blown laugh. It felt good to laugh.

"I missed hearing that," he whispered softly.

*I missed laughing.*

I turned away from the gatepost when we got to Raven Hill. He stopped right outside my house and I opened the door for myself before he could get out.

"Thank you, Declan. But..."

"I understand." He frowned as he closed his door.

"And you don't have to take care of—"

"I said I would and I will. Don't think of it as a favor. Think of it as a goodbye present or an 'I'm sorry' present…either one works." He handed me an envelope through the window.

"What is it?"

"You'll understand. Now go in before you scare your neighbors," he said and I glanced around to see a few people coming out.

"Bye."

"Goodbye, Coraline Wilson."

I wanted to stay, even knowing everything I knew, I didn't want him to go. But I took a step back and headed inside quickly. Resting my back against the door, I took a deep breath. Then, as I realized where I was, I bolted up the stairs.

"Imani!" I screamed.

"In here!" she called from her room.

Walking into her room, she had a suitcase on her bed, and she was busy throwing all of her things—*my things*—into it.

"What are you doing?"

"I already talked to Mom and Dad, I'm going to leave until this blows over."

"Imani, he died. There's not a wind in all the world strong enough to blow this over."

She froze as her brown eyes glanced at me, then she started packing faster.

"Imani!"

"What?!" she screamed as she threw a shirt into her bag. "Coraline, I was drunk and high! I will go to prison for like life! I can't, Cora."

"So what? You want me to take the fall for this? They think it was me!"

"They do?" She relaxed as she reached up to grab me. "Coraline, that's perfect—"

"In what way is this perfect?"

"Coraline, you're a model citizen. You have money. You'll be fine—"

I couldn't take it anymore. Just as I was about to slap some sense into her, a hand grabbed onto mine.

"What the fuck you thinking you doing?" Otis asked as he held onto me with his good hand. His face was still swollen, and there was a large bruise on the left side of his face.

"Let go and get out of my house." I tried to pull my hand from his grasp, but he held on tighter.

"Who the fuck do you think you talking to? Richie-rich?"

"Otis, it's fine."

"You better watch yourself, bitch." He sneered as he let me go.

Rubbing my wrist, I turned to her as she zipped up her bag. "I thought you both broke up."

"It was a misunderstanding." She smiled at him as he grabbed some more of her things—*my things.*

"Imani," I whispered trying to stay calm. "He's a gangster, an actual one. He needs to go—"

"Give us a few minutes, *princess,* and we'll both be out of here."

I tried to touch her, but she pushed my hands away.

"Imani, he will hurt you." I tried to reason with her.

"What do you know?" She pushed my shoulder on her way out. "Babe, I'm ready."

He nodded as he followed her out of the room.

I knew a lot more than I she thought. I knew how badly it felt to want to go and how badly you shouldn't. Watching them walk down the stairs I didn't know what to say.

"Babe, how much is that worth." Otis stopped to grab the Greek vase from the cabinet in the living room.

"Put it down." I rushed behind him.

"I've about had with you," he snapped at me.

"Otis, it belonged to her parents, just leave it." Imani pulled at his arm.

He kept glaring at me, and then he smiled. "My bad."

"No!"

He let drop out of his hands and it shattered as it hit the ground. I bent down and touched the larger pieces as Imani tried to pull him out the door. Taking a few pieces, I threw them at him. "You son of bitch!"

"You little cunt!"

He smacked me so hard I fell onto the ground, and as I tried to brace myself, I felt the shards of the vase bite deeply into my palms. "Who the fuck do you think you're talking to?"

"Otis, stop! Let's go."

"Imani, you step out that door with him, you are dead to me! I swear to God I will never forgive you." I wiped the blood from my corner of my eye.

"I don't need you, Coraline," she replied. "Otis, come on!"

But he stood there glaring at me until she came and pulled him back.

"Get out of my house!" I hissed at them.

Annoyed, he grabbed the entire shelf and pulled it down. It crashed right next to me, forcing me to back up quickly.

"Don't find yourself in Southbend, princess, or you might not be as lucky as you were today."

"GET OUT!" I screamed. "GET THE FUCK OUT!"

"Fuck you!" he shouted as they got into the car and drove off.

This couldn't be real. This couldn't be my life.

The envelope Declan had given me was on the ground. I hadn't let go of it until now thanks to Otis. Reaching for it, I broke the wax seal and dumped everything out onto the floor next to me.

Three passports.

9 black cards. No names. Just numbers.

One ticket to Greece.

And pictures. Our pictures together. Pictures we'd taken when we went zip-lining and swimming with the sharks. There was a note on one of the pictures.

*I don't want you to be afraid or chose me because you have no other choice. So run, Coraline. Keep having fun. My uncle will let you stay until tomorrow night. But if you stay past that, he will take you as a threat.*

*Thank you and be safe.*

*Declan.*

I noticed all too clearly that he didn't write 'PS. I love you' this time.

"What the hell happened?"

I glanced up as my uncle came inside.

"Your daughter killed someone, and then she ran off with her boyfriend. But not before he broke my mother's vase and got a good hit in."

He looked around the room in shock before looking to me.

"I heard about the accident from your aunt. It won't look good for the company if this gets out. We will lose clients. I know a guy at the police station, and for the right price he can make this look like a freak accident. Then we can donate to—"

"You're not going to ask me if I'm alright?" I questioned softly. "I'm covered in blood siting on the ground on. Shouldn't the first question you ask me be, 'are you all right?' If not as your niece, then at least as your ATM. Shouldn't that be the normal

239

reaction to this situation?"

He paused and I guessed it only dawned on him this wasn't okay. He looked me over as he opened his mouth and closed it again, like a fish.

"I'll give you the choice. Me or the bank."

"What?" He paused.

"Which one?"

"The bank," he replied without even having to think.

I nodded, not even surprised or hurt.

Ever since my parents died, I had been alone. Surrounded by people, but alone. What was the point in being a good person if you just ended up being run over by a bad one? Lifting up a picture of me in Cancun, I stared at myself. I'd been so happy then. It felt like it had been forever since that time, but it wasn't, it was still waiting for me. If everyone was going being to be selfish, if everyone was just going to do what they wanted anyway, then why couldn't I?

There were three choices in front of me.

Lifting the passport I stood up and walked past him.

"You really going to give it to me?" he yelled after me, but I didn't answer.

*First shower.*

*Then pack.*

# THIRTEEN

"Life has to end, she said. Love doesn't."

—Mitch Albom

# DECLAN

Two weeks.

You think I would've been over it. Over *her,* but once you knew what it was like to be truly happy, to feel like you were standing right next to the sun without getting burned, how can anyone go back to being in the dark?

"Declan?"

I glanced up at Evelyn. She and everyone else were staring at me. It felt like the first night when I came to live here. Everyone kept hovering over me at dinner.

"You alright?" she asked me kindly.

"He's fine," Sedric answered as he cut into his steak.

"I would prefer to hear it from him." She glared at him. She was the only one that could get away with that.

"I'm fine," I repeated.

"See?" Sedric chewed. "Let me know when she's gone."

"Of course." I nodded as I placed my fork down. "May I be excus—?"

"Master Callahan?" Our butler stepped into the dining room, arms folded behind his back.

"What is it, Samuel?" Sedric placed his fork down.

"There's a woman here for Master Declan," he said looking to me. "A Miss Coraline Wilson."

I got up so quickly that the chair fell over. I was out the door, knowing that Samuel wouldn't have let her inside without permission. The rain soaked my clothes, but I didn't care. She stood staring up at the house under a green umbrella, dressed in a peach-colored lace dress. A taxi was parked right behind her.

"Cora?" I grabbed her attention as I stepped in front of her.

She lifted the umbrella higher for the both of us to stand under.

"Hi." She smiled.

"I don't understand?" I was afraid to get too happy.

She pulled out a passport and handed it to me.

"You told me to have fun, but I don't know how to do that without you, so you're going to have to keep teaching me. I want stamps too."

I took the passport from her. But she needed to be sure.

"Coraline, I can't change who am or what I do—"

"I know. I'll do what everyone else does and look away. Is that good enough?"

All I could do was nod as I grabbed the sides of her face and kissed her the way I had dreamt of for the last two weeks. She kissed me back, but only shortly before breaking away. I noticed that one of her eyes seemed a little swollen. As I gently brushed my thumb against it, she winced.

244

"You're going to ruin my make up," she said softly.

"What happened to you?" I asked trying to stay calm in front of her.

"I'm fine—"

"Coraline, you being here means that you are mine. You are part of my family now. We don't hide our pain from each other."

She sighed. "Otis and I got into a fight when he left with Imani."

"Is everything alright out here?"

Turning back, Sedric stood at the door with his hands in pockets as his hard gaze shifted between us. I took both the umbrella and her hand before I led her up the stairs.

"Dad, this is my girlfriend, Coraline Wilson."

His eyebrow raised as he moved aside. "Welcome to Callahan Manor, Ms. Wilson."

"Thank you, sir." She stepped inside.

Evelyn, Neal, Olivia, and Liam all stood in front of the grand staircase and waited for Sedric to speak again.

"Ms. Wilson, this is my wife, Evelyn, I'm sure you remember her from the church," he stated as Evelyn walked forward.

"Of course she remembers me!" she said to him as she hugged Coraline. "Welcome, dear. You look beautiful."

"Thank you, ma'am—"

"Just Evelyn, we were in the middle of dinner. Have you eaten?"

"Not yet."

Evelyn frowned. "In this house, Coraline, we always eat dinner together. If I didn't force them to, they'd stuff their faces with fries and burgers until they died of heart attacks. Come now."

Coraline looked back at me and I nodded to her as she headed into the dining room. Olivia kissed Neal on the cheek before she turned and followed as well, leaving only the men in the front of the house.

Sedric stepped in front me. "She's yours now. Do you know what that means?"

I smiled as I nodded. "Protect, live, and die for her."

"I better not hear you say that you rushed into this later," he muttered as he squeezed my shoulder and headed back into the dining room.

"Dad," I called out and he froze before he turned to face me. "Otis of the Seven Bloods, he hit her. What *can* I do?" I knew he already had a plan for the Seven Bloods.

"After dinner you, your brothers, along with the rest of the clan, will pay a visit to Southbend. You know what happens to Mr. Emerson," he stated.

"Finally, something I'm good at," Liam said as he placed his arm around my shoulder. "I really can't deal with all this lovey-dovey shit. It's like watching Romeo and Juliet on repeat."

"Don't they die in the end?" Neal questioned.

246

Liam rolled his eyes. "Don't we all die in the end?"

"Well, while you two bitch, I'm going to go eat." I stepped into the dining room as a maid placed a plate in front of Coraline who had been seated right next to me.

Sitting down, she looked to me.

I took her hand and kissed the back of it. "I'm happy you're here."

"Me too."

"So, Coraline, where did you go to school?" Evelyn asked. I was sure she already knew the answer, Sedric had most likely done an extensive background check on her, but I was glad that she was trying to make Coraline relax.

She wasn't completely comfortable, but I knew that that would soon pass. It felt like just the beginning.

\*\*\*

She lay in the middle of my bed, and I wanted to just stare at her until the sun came up. Moving to her side, I kissed her cheek as I sat on the edge of bed.

"PS—I love you," she whispered, her eyes barely open.

"PPS—I love you more."

"Where are you going?" She sat up.

"An errand for my uncle." I didn't want to lie to her anymore.

Her mouth opened like she was going to say something, but

247

before she could, she closed it and lay back down.

"What's going to happen with Mr. Pierre?"

"The report will say that the brakes on your car weren't working, and that Mr. Pierre suffered a heart attack as he tried to help you get out. No one will question it."

"Okay. Please be safe out there," she whispered.

"Always," I promised as I kissed her cheek again. "I'll be back before the sun is up."

"I'll be here." She yawned.

She had no idea how wonderful it felt to know that.

Stepping out of my room, my uncle stood there already waiting.

"We're good Catholics. We can't have her living here and not married to you," he said as he handed me a small box.

Opening it, I saw a raindrop shaped diamond set in a white gold ring.

"It was your mother's."

"Thank you."

Just like that, he took it back and snapped it shut.

"Don't you have something to attend to first? You don't want to lose it in the chaos. You are taking Liam after all."

"See you when I get back," I said, already walking towards the back of the house.

When I got there, there were already four large black Jeeps waiting. Liam threw me a pair of gloves and a mask as I hopped up into the back of one of the Jeeps.

Placing the mask around my mouth, no one spoke as they pulled out. Slipping on the gloves, an AK-47 was handed to me. I checked the mag before I strapped it back in.

Taking out my second phone, I sent a mass text containing a photo of Otis. I wanted him alive so that I could kill the motherfucker myself. The men beside me were dressed in all-black and they nodded to me.

Southbend was the shithole of Chicago, stripped cars on blocks littered the streets, and the only people that came outside were junkies, pimps, hookers, and the people who were looking for any of the above. The police had basically given up on it. Which meant that a house could finish burning to the ground before anyone showed up.

The Seven Bloods had taken it over, and made themselves kings here. Maybe that was why they'd forgotten who fucking owned this city.

Patrick, who was in the lead car, parked and cut all the lights. The three other Jeeps copied him. I came out and stared up at the old, run-down house with the boarded up windows, and rusted front door. Walking up the worn-out wood stairs, I rang the doorbell and was somewhat surprised when it worked.

"Who in the fuck?" someone yelled before opening the door. He stood in an old pair of jeans that hung off his waist and a wife beater vest.

"Is Otis at home?" I asked kindly as I lifted the gun in my hand.

His eyes widened as he tried to make run for it towards the back, but I shot him twice before he could turn to run.

Two naked women ran out of the kitchen screaming.

"Otis!" I shouted as they hugged each other.

"Upstairs!"

The men behind me shot them as I made my way upstairs. One of his men came at me with a knife. Moving out the way, I grabbed his arm and flipped him onto his back as I shot him right in the stomach.

"Gun beats knife," I told him as I kicked in the first door. The man there reached for his gun, but I shot his arm and then his head.

When I turned around, Otis was standing behind me with a gun to my head. I pulled down the mask so that he could see my face and I dropped my gun. He grinned.

"You have no idea—"

Before he could finish, I twisted his hand and grabbed the gun. Using the back of it, I smashed it across his face, just as hard as I imagined he'd done to her. He staggered and crashed into the wall.

I fired at his knees and he went down, crying out like the bitch-ass motherfucker he was. "First lesson, if you're going to shoot. Shoot. Don't talk about it."

Grabbing his collar, I pulled him to the edge of the staircase before I kicked him down. He tumbled twice before he landed on top of the dead fuck at the front door. Picking up my gun, I walked down as Eric and another one of our men dragged him outside. I could see the smoke and hear the gunfire coming from the other houses around us, and as I looked up I could see that the night skies were tinted with the orange glow of the fires.

"This is the son of bitch that hurt my brother's girl," Liam said to the men who had circled in around us. Liam looked back to Otis who was being forced to stand on his two feet despite the bullets lodged in his kneecaps. "And what do we do to people who hurt our women?"

Handing the guns to Patrick, they forced his pants down as I walked to him.

"We turn them into women as well," I answered as he handed me a blade.

"No!" He struggled as I reached him and glared into his eyes.

"Did you feel like a big man when you hit her?" I asked him right before I made the cut.

He screamed so loud I was sure that his voice cracked twice, as the blood flowed.

"Second lesson, touch what is mine, you bleed."

Dropping his penis and testicles to the ground, they let him go and he passed out right next to them.

"OTIS!" Imani ran out of house towards him, but I grabbed

her and held her back as they poured gasoline on him. "Stop! Please Stop!"

They wouldn't.

Liam dropped the match and she screamed as she struggled against me.

"This. This is what happens when you turn a blind eye to your family," I hissed at her as I forced her to watch him burn.

She fell forward crying.

"What do we do with her?" Liam asked me. "Dad wanted this whole place *cleaned*."

"She's going to willingly check herself in at North Mount Psychiatric Hospital," I told him.

"No one *willingly* checks into North Mount," he replied.

"It's either that or West Ridge." At least she would be comfortable in North Mount.

He nodded and she struggled as the men grabbed her.

"Head home. You should at least spend the first night at the manor together."

"Thank you."

"Whatever," he muttered, already walking away.

He was a romantic at heart; I don't know why he tried to deny it.

# EPILOGUE

"And so, all the night-tide, I lie down by the side of my darling, my darling, my life and my bride."

—Edgar Allan Poe

# DECLAN

When I came out of the shower, she was sitting up in the middle of my bed staring at the ring I had slipped on to her finger while she slept.

"Too much?" I asked her as I leaned against the doorframe. "We can keep dating for a while if you'd like."

"It's just...wow. So much has happened in such a short space of time," she whispered as she twisted the ring around her finger. It was a little big, but I would fix that later. I liked seeing it on her.

Sitting on the bed, I took her hand and held it tightly.

"No more running?"

"I took your mother's money out of WIB. So yes, in the next ten years, it's going to be me and you." She smiled.

I leaned in and kissed her.

She fell back onto the bed as I hovered over her. "You and me until we are old and gray, Coraline *Callahan*."

## SEDRIC

Sitting on the edge of my bed, I pulled on the laces of my shoes when she hugged me from behind.

"She came back just as you said she would," I whispered. It was because of her that I'd allowed Coraline to have those two weeks. Evelyn had called it perfectly. "How did you know?"

"She reminded me of myself, and I came back." She kissed my cheek.

"I'm still trying to thank you for that," I replied as I held her hands in front of me.

"Do you think she'll make it with us? I don't want him to be hurt. They still have to visit Ireland, and you know how the clan feels about outsiders."

"Declan will protect her like you protected me. Like you've always protected me." She leaned down and kissed my head.

If that was the case, then just like she'd done for me, Coraline would keep him sane and grounded.

The wives...they were always the ones who gave us the strength we needed to keep going.

*"Protect, live, and die for her." It was the Callahan way.*

# ALSO BY J.J. MCAVOY

*Ruthless People Series*
RUTHLESS PEOPLE
THE UNTOUCHABLES
AMERICAN SAVAGES
DECLAN + CORALINE (a novella)

*Single Title New Adult Romance*
BLACK RAINBOW

# ABOUT THE AUTHOR

.J. McAvoy was born in Montreal, Canada, and currently studies humanities at Carleton University. As a child, she wrote poetry, where some of her works were published in local newsletters. J.J.'s life passion with literature has always been the role of tragic and anti-hero characters. In her series, *Ruthless People*, she aims to push the boundaries not only with her characters, but with also readers. She is currently working on a new adult contemporary romance entitled *Black Rainbow*, coming out in May, 2015.

http://iamjjmcavoy.com/

Made in the USA
San Bernardino, CA
13 August 2020